To MARY,

VIN, Vomen and VROom!

Love

Conor

LIFE AND DEATH

AND IN BETWEEN

This copy is number **516** of 750 printed.

18/11/04

First published 2004 by

Conor Bowman
8–10 Coke Lane
Smithfield
Dublin 7
Ireland

© *Conor Bowman 2004*

ISBN 0–9548403–0–5

Cover design by Úna Kavanagh
Typeset by Carole Lynch
Printed by Betaprint

Contents

∾

★(Water Pressure is an extract from an unpublished novel of the same name)

For

Sylvia, Hannah, Charlie, Dexter and Ruth

Christmas Eve in Memphis

~

It was Christmas Eve in Memphis. Over the cold macadam of Highway 51, running east past Graceland, the scent of snow gathered fifty feet above the road signs. The last-minute shoppers on Beale shuffled home with their hands full of wrapping and things they'd bought to give to people who didn't need them. Further out of town the university was deserted, like a large-hearted friend with so much to give but no-one around to share it with. A car raced past the General Post Office as the last light inside was switched off for the holidays. The street lights only just hid their envy from neon snowmen and sleighs clogging up the middle distance from just about everywhere. Five thousand miles away it was Christmas Eve too but a good bit later and certainly not Memphis. A police car raced past the General

Post Office in Dublin's O'Connell Street and the half-erected Millennium Spire advanced into the sky like an excited skewer.

"Will the door be open when I get back?" the man asked the clerk at the reception desk as he prepared to step out into the rain.

"It depends on when you get back," the clerk replied without any apparent trace of sarcasm.

"And if it's locked?"

"Then it will be opened by whoever hears the bell."

The man resisted the question which next came to mind. It was probably better to let the issue lie and to worry about it when he had to. *If* he had to. He felt the breeze wander up the steps into his face as he opened the door fully and stepped down onto the pavement turning up the collar of his overcoat as he did. A boy and a girl in their twenties walked by him holding hands. As they encountered a lamp-post some paces later they seemed to manage to continue without losing touch with each other although they walked one either side of the lamp post. He suspected that this was beginner's luck on a first date or else years of comfortable practice. He doubted it could be anything in between. The street was probably the widest in the whole country and he imagined it required a large number of pedestrians even to seem deserted. It was nearly nine o'clock now by the clock over Clery's Department Store and the models in the window displays leered in the half light with their masters and mistresses long since gone home to wrap gifts or practice their outrage for the inevitable rows at dinner tomorrow. In Memphis the boys would be gathering to exchange presents and to play touch-football in the flood-lit evening which was now gathering in. The DJ on the local station would be playing requests and someone would be chosen to phone in and request some song for the tenth time that day.

Across the street he saw the amusement arcade called Dr Quirkey's Good Time Emporium. The games and rides were switched off now and he presumed that the coins had long since been deposited so that the machines would go hungry for a few days. It had been a long time since he'd been in Dublin and he'd never been there for Christmas. It seemed the appropriate thing for this year though, given all that had happened. The faces of the people he passed seemed familiar and yet he knew that he knew none of them. They had a warm comfortable look which made them seem reassuring rather than threatening, or even neutral. He had not expected to find them so benign. The rain was less annoying than at home and he presumed that there was a degree of shelter afforded by the buildings them-selves. His coat glistened and he remembered how much of a Christmassy word that was. From his childhood the images of the Black and White Minstrels and the movie 'Holiday Inn' came rushing back up at him, like sickness and the memory of adorable sweets together sometimes might. He paused to look at a statue through the Post-Office window; an ancient warrior with a crow on his shoulder, the only way his enemies knew he was finally dead. Nothing would do them now only to step over the slaughtered pieces of their own friends to visit violence on the corpse, a stark contrast to their fear minutes earlier. Nothing would hold them back now from stealing forward in a knot like an embalmer, a drug dealer and the relatives' lawyer might converge on a corpse for one reason or another in modern times.

Seagulls wheeled and squeaked overhead and he looked up at them with no emotion. He remembered that the ocean was not very far away. At the end of the street the bridge jumped the Liffey and it flowed, on and out to the sea past the merchant ships in the docks and the naval vessel moored in the estuary. The river moved noiselessly and he turned left down the street with empty buses parked beside the pavement in a line. Further on, the vast sparkle of enormous cranes decked in red and blue Christmas lights held up the sky and drew a cheerful line beneath the moon. He walked and, as he did, the city dropped behind him and soon the only sound he was conscious of was the slap of his own footfall. Across a smaller bridge near one of the only tall buildings in town he walked, with Christmas around his shoulders like a cape which left him still cold.

Back in Memphis someone had driven down to the All-Night-Pharmacy at the Baptist Memorial to fill a pre-scription and they got caught in traffic coming back. The Fairgrounds had been booked from midnight to six thirty am and everyone was on edge as the afternoon drew to a close. When the merchandise arrived the mood changed and the party was "on" once again. They travelled in four cars to fool the couple of fans who had taken the night off from their families to keep watch at the gates through the wrought-iron musical notes. The security staff at the Fairgrounds were happy to work Christmas Eve and even happier to pick up the times five overtime check on their way home. The previous year one of them was given the keys to a new Cadillac for stopping the Ferris wheel and averting an accident-in-waiting created by unsafe wiring.

Along the south side of the river he watched lovers saunter up the boardwalk across the water and noticed the absence of public phone booths, now obsolete as the mobile phone caught everyone aware. A dog barked in a local-authority flat-complex courtyard as the restaurants slammed the bin-lids for the last time for days. He stopped outside the Clarence Hotel and smiled to himself and wondered where its owners from the band U2 were spending Christmas. Probably out in the suburbs with family and gold and platinum discs. He loved their sound and how it had been an anthem for him for twenty years now, in his car, at the beach, even on the night of the funerals. Branches of aerosol-snow-sprayed wood interlaced above the entrance to the hotel and through the double doors he saw a display of holly on the reception counter like a comforter on a cold night. The staff, in their grey uniforms with the collarless jackets, looked like the Beatles.

A car drove by and seemed to speed up just before it reached him to try and splash him from a puddle on the road. The water looped up and landed just short of his foot and he laughed and waved. The pedestrian lights were red so he crossed the street onto Capel Street Bridge. On the way up Capel Street a flashing sign in an "Adult" shop caught his eye. An array of products littered the window display and hinted at much more inside. Access was by ringing a bell and as he thought about pushing the buzzer the door opened and a small squat lady emerged carrying two shopping bags with the logo of a department store.

"Do you want something?" she asked with a tone which seemed destined only for negative replies. He shook his head and as he turned away he heard the clatter of the security shutter making contact with the ground. A policeman was searching a youth in a long green coat on the other side of the road outside an art gallery and the door of the squad-car was open out on to the street. Another cop sat in the passenger seat eating a bag of low-fat crisps.

The lights around the swimming pool had been turned on and the guys sat in deck chairs on both sides shooting at coloured Christmas-tree bulbs floating in the chlorine-scented water. The shots which missed slowed their way to the bottom of the pool while the smell of gunsmoke lifted into the air over the scene like reluctant fog. Somebody served a tray of sandwiches and, on a moon-shaped plate, a banana fritter with peanut butter and jelly waited for God to change out of his giant pyjamas. The tour was scheduled to begin on December 27th in Wichita and to end on New Years in Pittsburgh. The Voice were flying in for rehearsals on Christmas Day and although the piano player had threatened to quit, somehow everyone expected him to turn up.

It was nearly midnight when he walked back up the front steps of the Gresham Hotel. The door *was* open and the lights on the tree in the foyer seemed to welcome him into the space. The armchairs and settees were empty now and he collected his room key and was about to take the elevator when he heard the clink of glass from the residents' bar.

"A double Jameson with ice," he ordered. The boy behind the counter was fresh and happy looking. He was probably on overtime the man thought. Down at the other end of the counter two ladies in their 30's were having an argument;

"Well I *thought* it would be a treat, to have everyone here together for one bloody Christmas dinner." The speaker had a funny tint of red hair like highlights gone wrong. Her companion was a slightly slimmer version. They were almost certainly sisters.

"Well Barry's *not* coming. He says that Carol has a cold and she won't be better by New Year's Eve either."

"So it's you and me, and Jonathan and his lot and Annette and Daniel and…"

"And Mother…" the victim of highlighting finished her sister's sentence.

"And Mother…" she agreed.

"She's too old to cook for eleven…"

"Nine," her sister corrected.

"Alright nine then, but she's still too old."

"She wants us there and we've never all made the effort, so this year…"

"This year everyone except Barry and Sneezy will be making the effort."

7

"I'm going to bed Lorna, I'm absolutely wrecked. Next time we're flying direct to Shannon, not this Heathrow-Dublin nonsense."

"I couldn't get the flights."

"You would if you'd booked early enough."

Whatever remained in her glass was swallowed and she stepped down from the stool and kissed her sister good night by kissing her own fingers and patting her sibling's hair. The barman collected the empty glass and Lorna ordered another double Baileys with ice.

The man picked up his drink and walked the length of the bar and leaned in around her to see her face.

"Christmas goodwill starting early in your family?" For a moment he thought she was going to tell him what to do with himself. Something between them and the on-off lights behind them, reflected in the mirror in front of them, melted her mood.

"Twins," she said. "So alike we're completely different." She smiled as the drink arrived and he put money on the counter to pay for it.

"I'm a twin too," he said as she let him buy her the drink.

"And do you fight every Christmas?"

"I suppose we do if I'm honest about it."

"Will you be eating Christmas dinner together tomorrow?"

"No we won't. As a matter of fact I'll probably eat here in the hotel." She looked at him and he sensed that she had evaluated this response and given it the most favourable interpretation available; a statement of fact rather than a bid for sympathy.

"Well there are two free slots at my mother's house in Ennis tomorrow," she said with a grin.

"I know. I heard. Barry and Sneezy aren't travelling." They both laughed and she beckoned the barman and ordered another drink each and this time *she* paid.

"Do you have other family?" she asked.

He thought of opening his heart to her and telling about a car crash last May which had claimed the lives of his wife and their two children. He thought of telling her more than she could ever have needed or wanted to know; how he'd been to three pharmacies and had enough pills in his pocket to put himself asleep forever upstairs in this hotel or in the river at the end of the street.

"No, no I don't, I'd like to have had but it didn't work out that way."

"Oh."

They drank in silence and he looked at her hand for a wedding ring. He saw none. The man behind the bar hovered in a way which was designed to make them finish up and leave the bar. It did not have this effect on them. They sipped at each other, tasting snippets of the life and longings which comprised the people they were.

"What's your name?" she asked as the ice cubes clinked a warning that her glass was empty.

"Elvis," he replied. He waited for her disbelief ("You're joking, get lost, no your *real* name").

"Well happy Christmas Elvis, I'm Lorna," she held out her hand to him and perhaps even the promise of more if he was willing to reach out for it.

Back in Memphis it was seven o'clock and just beginning to snow. The cars in the drive waited for the exodus to the Fairgrounds. Upstairs, on an eight-by-eight bed, a gift sat wrapped on the silk cover. Inside the Fairgrounds the staff huddled around the old brazier and warmed their hands as the flakes hissed into the coals. One of the staff would be a Cadillac richer tomorrow but didn't know it yet. In Wichita the auditorium lay empty and ready and in Pittsburgh, New Year's Eve was already an hour closer than it was in Memphis. There were no cars on Highway 51 at that precise moment; just an empty space, four Cadillacs long, waiting for Christmas Day.

The Luckiest Boy in the Free World

~

The unfairness of the situation always amazed us but no matter how much anyone thought or hoped it would change it never did. She was an absolute stunner and her old man was a bastard and that was it really in a nutshell. At sixteen years of age she fetched and carried and ran and ran back at his whim; to the bookie's shop on the corner, to the post office on the main street and even to the train station every afternoon at precisely four thirteen to get the evening paper for him as it arrived, before the local shops got a look in.

She was tall for her age but almost boyishly shy, in that way in which the eldest child of a family often is in the company of adults. The thin line of her smile, when she smiled, was like something so sharp you could have cut your throat with it but she radiated serene, gorgeous, youthful beauty with every step she took or word she spoke. She had a Kildare accent which was really more North Wicklow or West Dublin because it was devoid of the harsh "dis dat dese dem and dose" signature sounds of the locality. She was in fifth year in the convent and absolutely everybody in the collateral year in Newbridge College boys' boarding school was stone cold in love with her. Especially me.

Raymond Mockler, her father, was a huge man who had hands like shovels and a heart as cold as a grave he might have dug himself with those same hands. They lived in a small terraced house off the back street, a home so tiny it was as though the housing authority had deliberately matched man and mortar just for the comic value of this absurd union. He did not work, his wife was dead and all he had was a daughter who was so unlike him in every way that it was unfair to both of them. He shouted; she spoke softly. He drank; she barely ate. He was violent and she had once been seen by Fizzer Kelehan helping a field mouse up onto the path on the Milltown Road. Sometimes she went to school with her eyes down to the ground like a puppy no one wants and sometimes she stayed away from school altogether but returned when the bruises had reduced to a level beneath the interest of the Gardai or the doctor. Things were explained with the kind of excuses we all expect to rail against in disbelief and concern when we hear them but never do; "I fell"; "the hot-press door"; "the corner of the shelf on the landing." The tales of her mistreatment filtered through the hand-holding unions of the fifth-years from both schools, past the stolen kisses in the lane behind

Murtagh's shop and down into my school satchel, army-green and covered in homage to Arsenal and the Stray Cats, to where I could relive and rehear their horror every time I made a heart and filled in the words "I love Celine."

'Why don't you go to the door and knock on it and fucking have him?' Tommy Ryan said to me one day in double-geography as we discussed the unfair domestic conditions of this girl neither of us knew.

'I will I will, just give me a chance.' But I never did.

We grew up, or at least we got bigger and moved into the last year of the school cycle, itching to get out of our uniforms and into the real world. The irregularity of French verbs haunted us to sleep as the Leaving Cert approached and every edgy response, to the pressure which threatened to erupt, saw us play out Macbeth unwittingly in the refectory with burnt toast and the hint of sunshine luring us outside into the quadrangle. I hadn't seen her for months and then one day, while I wasted an afternoon on the Space Invaders machine in Riozzi's Take-away, I saw her reflection in the screen as she came in looking for potato scallops and a tin of 7-Up. It was a moment to cherish forever as she saw me watching her and smiled so that we met in a second-hand way in the glass of the machine. I deliberately lost my way in the hunt for invaders and got off the stool and decided to be hungry enough for chips. We both reached for the red tower of ketchup together and her hand touched mine and we looked at each other in that way in which you just *know*.

'Biology tomorrow,' she announced with a smile and I remembered that she too was in the middle of exams. I walked her to the end of the street. Neither of us wanted to go where we were supposed to, so we turned in the opposite direction and made for the river. I don't know how it happened (perhaps even as predictably as when we were crossing the road) but we held hands and when we were halfway along the tow-path I turned and told her my name.

'I'm Jimmy, Jimmy Liston.'

'I'm Celine,' she said offering her right hand and we shook on our introductions. She didn't tell me her surname and although I knew it already I asked her what it was.

'It's not *my* surname, it's his,' she said simply.

'Whose?'

'Me Da's.'

She turned away and tugged my hand so that I went with her, down along by the river with the water slapping by us going in the opposite direction. We were two people on the brink of the world who should have been cramming our hopes down onto foolscap paper and praying the exams would go well, but those kind of days only sandwiched that afternoon as we walked and walked as far away from our lives as we could until the town was out of sight.

'Where are you going next year? Back to Galway I suppose?' she said casually as we sat and pulled the heads of long grass stalks through our fingers before setting the grains on their way in the water.

'I'm supposed to go to University, law or medicine or something but…'

'But it's not what you really want is it?' she finished my sentence in a question back at me which made me re-think

14

the whole thing as if the answer lay in the grasp of the boy in the mirror and not with me at all. I think I only spoke after I was sure she would not laugh at my dream, although in truth I cannot be certain that I had that security before I opened my mouth.

'I want to be singer, or a writer, some bloody thing that's different and new and challenging. Anything except... except...' I was unsure of the words I wanted to say.

'Anything except what's expected?' she posited and that was the magic combination of words I'd felt in my heart for so long.

'Yes,' I said. 'You've hit the snail on the shell.' We both laughed, easy in each other's company.

She wore faded denims and a Kildare football jersey and on her feet were the kind of sandals monks wear. Her hair was mousy brown with streaks of blonde where the sun had tried to be unkind but had failed. But it was her eyes, especially when she smiled, which made her seem fragile and gentle and as beautiful as a butterfly. Those eyes were the colour of the sea on every holiday programme which ever featured destinations you could never afford. She was truly truly beautiful and I have to say that I knew myself to be the luckiest boy in the Free World to be there with her on that afternoon beside the Liffey.

I wanted to ask her about her father and to tell her all I knew about her situation (or at least suspected second-hand) and of how all the boys in my class had boasted at one stage or another that they would right the wrong but none of us had. It was crazy, I told myself, to be preparing to launch into self-righteous clap-trap like that when I had no earthly right in the whole world to do so. We'd shared tomato ketchup and chips and walked for an hour but beyond that, I warned myself, I had absolutely no place telling her what I thought was wrong with her own life. For the first time of real consequence I thought before I spoke and avoided speaking as a result. We watched the water in silence and then, in a brave moment, I took her hand and kissed it and she let me. I wondered if this were the time to be a bit braver but she beat me to it and kissed me on the lips as she sprang to her feet and said with a mischievous grin,

'Race you!'

She undid her sandals and then took them off and buckled them together for more weight and whirled them around her head before letting go in mid-twist so that they sailed through the air and landed on the other bank. I was only beginning to get my own black "Clarke's Best" off when she ran to the edge of the river and dived in. I saw the early evening sun shimmer over her as the lily-white jersey sought the safety of the bend and her bare feet kicked towards the bank she'd abandoned, propelling her in the direction of the small ruined Norman tower on the other side. I threw my own shoes one at a time but the first one didn't make it and sank like a stone so I let the other one follow it. What use is one shoe? My grey shirt and flannel trousers were not exactly waterproof but in I went and I thrashed about until I found some pattern of movement and began to make progress. As I gulped down a mouthful of what I hoped was pure mountain stream I saw her reach the other side and pull herself up onto dry land.

We lay on the grass for what seemed a pleasurable eternity as our clothes half-dried on a hedge while a thin vapour of steam rose from them and climbed above us up at the sky. It was just one of those days when everything seems right and you manage to appreciate it as it happens. The happy sound of the river and the occasional "awk" of a crow or magpie were the only reminders to us that there was anything else in the world apart from ourselves that June afternoon. I closed my eyes at one point and yet I still knew, from the shadow which passed over me, that when I opened them she would be there with me, watching and waiting, and she was, leaning her chin on her hands and her elbows resting on the grass supporting her.

'Hello,' she smiled when I returned from my moment's nap.

'Hello yourself,' I grinned. As I tried to sit up she was as close as could be and I was unable and now unwilling to move ever again. She tickled my nose by blowing lightly at me and then we kissed and stayed like that for hours talking and being tender and completely forgetting about things like the Leaving Cert or her father's evening paper or my shoes.

At about nine that evening I walked her to her house and a lady opened the door as we arrived up the short path.

'Oh Celine, there you are.' She put her hands to her face. 'We were worried sick.'

'Where's me Da Mrs. Gallagher?' I saw movement behind the lady in the hall as another woman with a sweeping brush in her hand emerged from the kitchen.

'Is it Celine?' the second lady called out. Mrs. Gallagher waved her hand for silence.

'And who's this?' Mrs. Gallagher said looking disapprovingly at my bare feet as she retreated into the house pulling Celine with her. 'From the College I suppose?'

'Where's me Da?' Celine repeated. I heard the word 'hospital' being whispered and then the door slammed.

I sat my biology exam the following day confident in the knowledge that I was going to fail but that it would be worth it for the time spent in her company. I couldn't stop thinking about her and I wanted to be with her all of the time and to know how she was and whether she felt the same now as she did then, because I knew I did. Every waking moment found my mind filled with her face. I heard her voice in the whisper of every leaf which rustled on the edge of the playing fields and in each passing snippet of conversation thrown my way by the architectural foibles of the echoing corridor outside of empty classrooms.

Scanning the obituary column, after I'd finished my exam, there was no sign of her father. Later that afternoon I walked to her house and rang the doorbell and steeled myself for a confrontation with him if he answered and wanted to know how I dared call for his daughter. The buzzer sounded in the space behind the door but no one answered. I wrote a note and addressed it to her and sent it registered post with my last few coins two days before I was due to leave for home. I told her the time of the train and that I missed her.

On the morning of the day I was leaving I called to her house, again with no luck, then walked up and down the main street in the hope of bumping into her. There was a seriousness about the end of June which told me I was on my way. I did not know the destination but the journey began as I packed my things in the dormitory and took my posters down from the cubicle walls, lifting odd shapes of paint with Blu-tac as I did. I had a one-way ticket to Galway and so I waited for the train. I remembered how the situation with her father had always struck me as unfair. What was I to make of my own situation now? Had Celine Mockler moved on to someone else? Was she on the tow-path by the river wearing the same sandals? What was the story with her father? Who had those women been and what had they done with the girl I loved? Had she got my note? The train moved off, leaving four years of my life behind.

As we made our way across the Curragh minutes later I saw her up ahead standing beside a water-pump, her father's "High Nellie" bicycle leaning against the stone trough. She was holding a piece of paper in her hand and waving it frantically. I leaped to my feet and pulled the emergency cord. The train slowed down with a ferocious squeal of metal on metal and I began to walk to the nearest carriage door holding on to the headrests of other people's seats as I did. I could see a railway official in a uniform making his way through the interconnecting door of the carriages ahead and my choices narrowed. I pushed down the window and reached out to grab the door-handle. A shout of 'Hey you' followed me as I jumped on to the grassy bank and rolled down startling a couple of grazing sheep as the train finally stopped. Out of the windows passengers gazed and laughed and clapped as the girl on the bicycle approached and I ran beside her until I was able to hop onto the crossbar. I looked behind and saw two men scrambling down to the level of the road where their futile cries were carried away on the wind. When we were safe we stopped and dismounted from the bike. As she began to formulate the words of explanation I kissed her and held her as tightly as I could, never wanting to ever let her go.

Water Pressure

~

"You've drowned him."

"No I haven't."

"You bloody-well have."

"No way. He's spoofing."

"If he's spoofing why hasn't he come back up?"

"If he's drowned why isn't he dead?"

It was June. The summer stretched out ahead of them like an avenue lined with stolen dreams and forbidden fruit. For Charlie Caulfield, Augustine Cahalane and Harry Doherty this summer was going to be the best ever. School would be out for three months the following week and they had plans. They were fourteen years of age and bursting to grow up. Mutter's Bridge had always seemed to belong to them and the narrow ledges beneath its arches hid them from the world. A grey stone canopy over their heads and the real taste of summer; it was perfect.

"I'm telling you, you've drowned him." Augustine sounded worried.

"Charlie's well able to swim, he won the County Cup for us last year against Saint Brendan's remember ?" Harry Doherty was the taller of the two and he craned his neck out over the rushing water and balanced himself by pushing his fingertips up against the cold underside of the bridge.

"The current here is mad." Augustine crawled on all fours, his gaze following the flow of the river round the corner of Bowler's Meadow and on into the town.

Harry knew Charlie Caulfield too well to be unduly concerned. All he'd done was push him in. There was no way he could have come to any harm. It wouldn't be the first time any of them had been in the river, especially not Charlie.

"Let's go up around by the path to Bowler's. I bet he swam there and got out." Harry knew everything was alright. It was just a joke, Caulfield acting the goat. He'd kill him when he caught up with him, the bastard.

"There are millions of reeds here," said Augustine.

"See what did I tell you? Caulfield you bollix, come on out and show yourself." Harry swung a hazel branch at the reeds like a sword. There was no sign of Charlie. He was probably hiding on the other side of the river trying to unnerve them.

"He's not here," said Augustine. "I'm telling you he wouldn't have been able to swim this far." There was real fear on Augustine's face and if Harry had turned around and seen it he would have been afraid too. If it *was* a joke then Augustine certainly wasn't in on it. They walked slowly back along the river to the bridge and stared at the water minutely as though able to see through it. Here and there tiny spools of bubbles indicated rainbow trout but, beyond that, there was little they could see from the bank.

"Look, look Harry," Augustine pointed in a panic out into the middle of the river. Harry glanced left in time to see a tiny swirl.

"What? What?"

"It was a shoe, a shoe, I saw it, a shoe, Charlie's shoe."

"Fuck off, it was some sort of fish, it could have been anything." Harry knew that Augustine was an exaggerative type at the best of times. This was simply panic going into overdrive or else an elaborate hoax. Whatever else had happened, or whatever Augustine Cahalane thought he'd seen, Charlie Caulfield hadn't drowned and no-one had just seen one of his shoes. Harry was certain of that.

"One of us should jump in Harry."

"You mean *I* should ?" Harry smirked.

"Well *I* didn't push him in and anyway I can't really swim."

"And I didn't drown him," said Harry firmly.

"I'm going home," said Augustine. "We have to tell someone."

"There's nothing to tell, Charlie's probably at home himself right now getting changed and laughing his head off at the pair of us. Don't tell anyone, I'm warning you. All we have to do is sit tight and Charlie Caulfield will come round some corner soon. Don't be an eejit. Okay ?"

Harry was much less confident than he sounded but it was important not to flinch. Even the slightest sign from him that he was worried would mean the whole thing had worked. He couldn't be sure whether or not Augustine was in on it, possibly not, but all the same any betrayal of his own worry in front of him would provide the proof Caulfield needed to slag him off for the rest of the summer. No way. He wasn't going to catch Harry Doherty out.

"See you Augustine." He waved nonchalantly as they parted at the T-junction with the accident black spot sign. Harry threw a stone at the sign like someone trying to tempt a water-tanker into Hell. It made him feel better.

Cattle-grids were useless. There was a stray cow in his mother's flowerbeds and it took Harry and his dad ages to get it out. It was like one of those old films where there were four or five doors out into the same corridor and no-one was able to catch anyone else. The cow darted around the garden using the low hedges as shelter from its pursuers. Harry was exhausted when they finally got it out through the side gate. They threw stones after it to make it bolt off down in the direction of McHenry's shop. Mrs McHenry wouldn't be long throwing a few stones after it herself.

"How are the lads?" his father asked as they caught their breath.

"Not too bad." It was the first time since he'd got home that he'd remembered the river. He couldn't have drowned Caulfield? Surely not?

"We'd better go in," his father nodded in the direction of the kitchen window where Harry's mother was mouthing silently that the tea was ready.

"I hope that cow didn't make too much of a mess?" she inquired when they had sat down at the large pine table in the kitchen.

"No Ma, we got it out before it could do any damage."

"Where's it gone now ?"

"Mrs McHenry's Shop," they answered together and started laughing. This was good; looming school holidays, brown bread, hot steaming tea and his Dad laughing his head off.

"Can I use the phone ?" Harry slipped it into the conversation between scones.

"Sure," said his dad.

"Not too long now Harry, mind my phone bill," his mother smiled.

"I'm afraid Charlie's not here at the moment."

"Oh." A knot in Harry's stomach pulled his insides apart.

"Wasn't he with you this afternoon Harry ?"

"Er, yes Mrs Caulfield, he was, but we were only down by the bridge for a while then we came back through the village."

"That's strange because he wasn't home for his tea."

"Oh, was he not ?" Harry tried to sound calm and surprised.

"No sometimes on a Saturday he takes the bus to Moynalvy to see his grandad. He's not too well at the moment."

Harry was relieved, Caulfield was trying to draw out the joke to really get him worried. Well he could fuck off for himself.

"When do you expect him back ?"

"I don't know really Harry, sometimes he stays over. The last bus back gets in at eight so if he's not on that he's probably staying."

"Could you give me his grandad's number Mrs Caulfield?" He'd call him up and give him a bollocking down the line that would redden the post mistress' ears, the old bitch.

"He doesn't have a phone Harry I'm afraid. Can I take a message and I'll get Charlie to ring you tomorrow?"

"Oh no thanks Mrs Caulfield. It's not important at all. In fact don't even tell him I rang."

"Are you sure ?"

"Definitely Mrs Caulfield, listen thanks anyway." He wasn't going to give Caulfield the satisfaction of knowing he was worried. He'd let Charlie sweat it out as well.

The flicker of O'Malley's television in the sitting room across the road reminded Harry of lightning. He stared out the window of his bedroom with his chin propped up on his hands. His elbows buzzed with sensation through the thin window sill as hailstones began to pelt at the glass. Hailstones in June. What was going on? A car sped down the road with its lights on and Harry wondered if the seasons had gone crazy. Then, without warning, it stopped. It was as though the weather had forgotten itself for a moment and was now back to normal. A poster of the county football team on his wall caught the rays of the sunset over his shoulder and, for the first time that day, Harry Doherty was actually afraid. He had gone down to the station to meet the bus from Moynalvy but Caulfield wasn't on it. He phoned Caulfield's home from the kiosk outside the post office.

"I'm sure he's staying with his grandad. Do you want me to give him a message Harry? He'll be here in the morning."

Harry caved in. "Okay so Mrs Caulfield, could you get him to eh…" he struggled for words.

"To phone you is it?"

"Yes, yes, to phone me, please get him to ring, just a quick call."

"Is everything all right Harry ?"

"Oh yeah Mrs Caulfield, not a bother, see ya." Now Charlie would definitely win.

It was ridiculous, this knowing but not knowing. It was like going back to check the door was locked when you knew that you already knew it was. Caulfield was an expert when it came to scamming it or trying to worry others. Harry remembered Charlie in school getting himself and Cahalane to set up victims. The deal was that Harry or Augustine would tell some unsuspecting classmate that Charlie's older sister had won the World Irish Dancing Championship the previous weekend. When the innocent victim approached Charlie to congratulate him Charlie would break down and pretend with a mixture of anger and hurt that his sister had just lost both her legs in a car accident. Charlie didn't have a sister and Harry wondered if he even had a conscience. Harry knew he hadn't drowned him. Charlie was out there somewhere laughing at him.

Well he wouldn't psych Harry Doherty out. Christ, why didn't he phone? This had gone too far. Where was he?

Harry awoke in the middle of the night. There was no phone at Charlie's grandad's house so he couldn't phone home to say where he was. But what about the clothes? He caught sight of his own jeans thrown over the back of a chair and his mind raced. Charlie's clothes would have been soaking wet, he hardly got on the bus with wet clothes? No, no, of course he didn't, he'd have lain in the sun at the top of Bowler's Meadow and let them dry out on a wall and then taken the bus to Moynalvy. Charlie always had change in his pockets, that wouldn't fall out in the water. That was it; he'd dried his clothes and taken the bus. But why didn't he phone home from a phone box? There was no need really as his mother seemed sure enough of his whereabouts. Therefore he would probably guess that Harry might phone later on if he got worried (not that Harry *was* worried) and his mother would put Harry's mind at ease by saying Charlie had gone to his grandad's. Harry lay awake cross-examining himself. Why this? What if? But surely? He finally fell asleep again but awoke on Sunday with a vivid memory of a nightmare in which Charlie's drowned face looked out at him through a glass wall in an aquarium as brown shoes sank slowly all around his body gradually burying him.

"I'm telling you Harry, I don't know anything about it, I swear."

Harry held Augustine by the collar of his short-sleeved shirt up against the back wall of the church after Mass.

"Look Augustine, if you know what's going on then tell me. Where *is* Charlie?"

"I don't know, I swear on my life I don't know. Look Harry, let's tell someone, they must be worried sick about him at this stage. What if…?"

"Shut up Cahalane." Harry pushed him back against the wall as he let go his grip, "If you're in on this I'll fucking well kill you. Charlie is fine, he's holding out on us that's all." Neither of them really believed it.

Harry waited in the front room all afternoon for the telephone to ring. He longed to hear Charlie Caulfield's voice, he needed to know that he was still right, that it *had* all been a hoax. He was willing to trade anything at this stage for the reassurance that Charlie was safe. He wondered if it was too late to cut a deal with God. Harry's mother went for her usual Sunday stroll down to the ruined castle on the Dublin road and back, while his father listened to Tipperary beating Limerick on the radio. Why didn't Charlie bloody-well ring or something? At half time his father went out to the shed to smoke a cigarette having given them up twelve years before. Harry dialed the number of Caulfield's house. He held the receiver to his ear and the 'parp-parp' down the line told him there was no-one home. Surely his mother would be there or something? She hardly ever seemed to leave the place since Charlie's dad had died a few years earlier.

Worry gave way to outright fear and Harry finally decided to surrender altogether. He wheeled his bike out the front gate and set off for Milltown where Charlie lived.

It was four miles out the road but this was the only way to set his mind at ease. He wished he'd been strong enough not to give in but Augustine's attitude that morning had set alarm bells ringing. He pushed over Mutter's Bridge and looked down from the road into the river. The water thinned into the middle distance and swept away towards Dublin. Charlie was a good swimmer. Wasn't he?

The door bell echoed in the hall of Caulfield's house on the other side of the opaque glass in the front door. Harry rang it six times but there was no reply. He walked around the back of the house and rapped on the door of the kitchen. Silence. Blast. As he walked slowly down the avenue towards the main road he felt as though he were being watched but this was now more a vain hope than a legitimate expectation.

"You're not very hungry Harry." His mother cleared away the plates from the table after tea. Harry didn't reply.

"Are you all right Harry? You look a bit pale." His father folded the Sunday paper and leaned back in his chair.

"Huh ?" Harry snapped out of his daze.

"Is everything all right Harry?" his father repeated.

"Yes, yes everything's fine, I'm just a bit tired that's all. I probably need an early night."

"Well, not too long to go now," his mother smiled gently. "You'll be on holidays on Wednesday."

Holidays, Wednesday, school, tomorrow. It was still bright when Harry went to bed. He'd rationalised the whole thing now. Caulfield had got back from Moynalvy and had gone out visiting somewhere with his mum for the afternoon. That was all that had happened. Keep it simple, that's what Mr. Butler the Biology teacher always said. He was referring to exams. Well this was a sort of exam, a bloody test. In fact he had already decided what he was going to do tomorrow at school when he saw Charlie in class. He would pretend that nothing had happened and that everything was as normal. He wouldn't ever refer to the river incident because that would only provide Charlie with the chance to embarrass him in front of the rest of the lads. No, keep it simple, pretend nothing had happened and *then* beat Charlie up.

"Where *is* Charles Caulfield?"

The shrill voice of Miss Ryan, their English teacher, cut through the half-nine madness like a whiplash. A vague look of despair took over her face and then she gazed around the class again and relaunched the question. Missing her class was an affront and only those with the very best of reasons ever dared. A dentist's appointment was not acceptable as an excuse and nuclear war would only have been borderline.

"I said - Where is Charles Caulfield?"

No-one replied and yet there was a palpable murmur amongst the raggle taggle collection of fourteen year-olds which buzzed into Harry's head like a needle filled with venom. He couldn't believe it at first but the hum translated inside his ears, and he now knew, or at least accepted, what he had always feared. He scanned the class for a friendly face but all he met were blank hateful stares. They knew, they knew. He turned his head away from the body of the class and Augustine Cahalane was facing him across a secondhand copy of Macbeth mouthing in slow motion as he made a slashing gesture across his own neck.

"He's dead, he's dead, Charlie's dead."

The next few seconds blurred into one as Harry rose to his feet and fought his way across through a sea of army-green schoolbags on the floor the classroom.

"Where are you going? Where are you going?" Miss Ryan's voice chased him along the corridor past the Science labs and down the chessboard-tiled stairs to the front hall of the school lined with class photographs. He raced across the quadrangle past the Morris Minors and Anglias like abandoned tanks at the Somme and on toward the wrought iron gates which opened the world to Saint Xavier's Secondary School for boys. Down the tarmac avenue like a racehorse his legs pumped and his head filled with horrible images of Charlie's face in an aquarium. A torn shoe in the gutter at the bottom of the hill up to Mrs McHenry's shop was like a sign from God that he hated Harry Doherty. He had to get home and tell his parents. His dad would understand, his mother would protect him, his bedroom would hold him safe and warm from the world like a big blanket. He fell while running up the hill and his hands shredded on the road the Corporation had resurfaced the previous April. Mrs. McHenry's face stared out the window past the humming HB ice cream machine and her eyes were filled with wonder. Harry stumbled on and up toward his own house like a wounded bird half-crazed with hunger and fear. "Charlie Caulfield, Charlie Caulfield," the hedges chanted as he fell past and the small pool of water in the trench beneath the cattle-grid mirrored his face like a man staring out a prison window into the rain.

At five-past midday his mother returned from shopping. Minutes later Charlie Caulfield sauntered up Doherty's avenue to tell Harry the good news. He was an hour and a half, a rope and a garden shed too late.

The Chess Men

The Chess Men

~

For years, longer than any of them could remember, the three of them had gathered every Wednesday night at eight o'clock to play chess. Each week it was a different house, where a different wife made three cups of tea and a basket of sandwiches and received little thanks other than three incomprehensible mutters.

This was their night. They kept it apart from the rest of their lives, allowing no one to intrude and everyone in the village soon came to accept it. If someone needed a doctor or a policeman, or a prescription filled, on a Wednesday night they had to look elsewhere. Only in cases of emergency would any of the three be disturbed and it rarely happened.

It was a ritual; the two visitors would arrive at the host's house at exactly five minutes to eight. When the coats had been hung under the stairs and the pipes had been lit, the clanging of the church bell would accompany the setting up of the pieces and the choosing of the first two players. They were chosen by placing three pawns (two white and one black) in the leather case which housed the chess set. The host selected first, with his eyes closed, then the host from the previous week, and the third person was left with the remaining pawn. Those drawing the white pawns played first, their colours decided by repeating the process with one pawn of each colour. After that, the winner always changed colours for the next game.

The person who was not playing acted as referee, although disputes rarely arose because all three men fully understood the game and its rules. When they had been younger, desperation had occasionally driven the doctor to cheat because the other two were much better players than he, however over the years this inequality of ability had evened out and refereeing became superfluous to all intents and purposes. Perhaps now they all knew each other too well to be surprised in the course of a game and increasingly each game was now very much anybody's for the winning. For a time the third man had recorded all of the moves in a hard-backed ledger but this practice had been abandoned. None of them remembered when or why. They kept their own notes of course and discussed each game when it finished.

John Reilly had come to Castletown fresh from Templemore; a raw police recruit sent down the country to learn his profession under the watchful eye of Sergeant

Flynn, who at the time was in his early forties. A couple of years later Flynn had been transferred to Dublin and Reilly had been made Sergeant in his place. He went about his business in a casual way which endeared him both to the locals and to his superiors and he was pretty much left to his own devices as a result. He had married a local girl and they had three children, all grown up now and with lives of their own, the two girls nursing in England and the boy, Seamus, a sales rep for Guinness. Now in his thirty-fourth year in the village, Reilly felt very much at home and at ease. His duties were regular and unchallenging apart from the occasional check-point after a robbery in Galway and the twice-yearly inspection by a Superintendent from Dublin. He was content.

The games were keenly contested and for the most part did not take much longer than half an hour each. The fact that someone was always waiting to play the winner discouraged delay and on the odd occasion when a game strayed over the half hour nobody really minded. They never played past half-past eleven which meant that six or seven games were as many as could be managed in an evening's play. The winner was permitted to stay on up to a maximum of three consecutive games, which ensured that they all played each other at least once. The last game always ended at eleven thirty and no matter what the state of play at that point an end was declared and the player with the most captured pieces was the winner. The pieces were valued in points ranging from twenty for a queen down to one for a pawn. It had been decided that this was a better way to end rather than declaring a draw as it forced the last two players of the evening to play attacking chess and take risks.

On the basis of one point for a win, and half a point in the case of stalemates, they kept a note of the results of the evening's play. The winner each week was stood a pint by the other two on Saturday night when the three met up in Finan's Bar in Barrack Street at about 10 o'clock. Bill Finan knew the three men well and for almost as long as they had been playing chess together he had been serving the winner two pints on a Saturday night at the expense of the others. He was never short of a moment to chat to them and even on a busy night, when he had other staff behind the bar, he insisted on serving the chess men personally. He usually managed to accompany his service with a comment or two;

"Kevin you're doing well this weather what? You must be taking valium instead of selling it," or;

"Well Doc you're getting a taste of your own medicine this week."

Whenever Sergeant Reilly won Bill Finan would wink at him and say jokingly,

"You're in good form tonight, enjoy your pint – I'll have the place cleared in time for opening in the morning, all I need is ten minutes to wipe the tables." This was a reference to the draconian pub-opening hours in Ireland.

In a way the three men lived a life apart from the rest of the inhabitants of Castletown. They were professional men drawn together by a combination of factors; an interest in chess; the size of the community but, most of all, by their positions in the village. In the company of each other they were on first name terms of course, however to everyone else they all had titles: Mr. Fahy; Doctor Cooke; Sergeant Reilly. This placed them slightly ahead of the rest of the village, indeed only the Parish Priest ranked above them in the local professional hierarchy and that was because even they looked up to him. He would always be "Father Mitchell," no matter how well they knew him. They had once considered expanding their number to four to even-up things on a Wednesday night but decided against it as Father Mitchell was the only suitable candidate and they felt it would be unwise to invite the intimacy such a choice would entail. If the truth be known this was roughly the same reason for which they themselves were never invited to whist drives or bingo games in the village. Perhaps they would not have gone even had they been invited.

In a way their decision to keep their number at three was also half-prompted by a fear of rejection and the inevitable awkwardness that then would follow between themselves and the priest. The village, like any community larger or smaller, consisted of niches and tiers. Most people seemed content with the niche they had found or had been allocated and while everyone complained about everyone else, either higher up or lower down on the ladder than themselves, it was never out of a desire to swap places.

Adrian Cooke was a native. His father had been the Master at the local National School and he had grown up with a keen sense of the importance of education. It had been hammered into him at home, both physically and verbally, and as a result he had gone on to study medicine at U.C.D. He remembered the gin parties and the two girls in the class outlasting most of the boys at the first anatomy practical. One of his clearest memories was of rounding a corner on his bike on the morning of his graduation and seeing a large group of people eating cake and drinking champagne in the small garden of a terraced house. It was the house of a man called Emilio Scallan; the first winner of the Irish Sweepstake. Doctor Cooke had been semi-retired for years and was the eldest of the three chess players. A few mornings a week he saw patients in his surgery. He made the occasional house-call but most of the locals went to a younger doctor who was just establishing himself in the area. Doctor Cooke didn't mind the competition as it had allowed him to scale down his own practice and feel retired and useful at the same time.

Occasionally the three entered competitions as a team. Not so much now but in the seventies. They had travelled as far afield as Claremorris and Birr to take part in round-robin Tournaments. Once they had entered the National Championships when they had been held in an hotel in Salthill. Roughly fifty teams had entered and a team from Galway had won. Castletown hadn't made it past the first round; they were beaten 2-1 by Moate. Kevin Fahy had been their only winner and it was a great source of satisfaction to him and made him "the man to beat" within the group for a couple of months afterwards. However he often wished secretly that he had lost as well as he felt that it had driven a small wedge between him and the other two, although nothing was ever said. That was over twenty years ago now and had been nearly forgotten because they never played anyone except each other anymore. They were too old to travel around and perhaps not as sharp as they used to be.

The chemist shop on Main Street had been Fahy's for almost half a century. He had moved to Castletown after working in London for the first few years after qualifying. His wife and he had met there when she was a nurse during the war. Business had grown over the years and he now had two girls working full-time in the shop with him. He worked in the shop six days a week, shutting for a half day Wednesday and Saturday like Blackrock College where he had been to school. The half days then had been for the purpose of playing rugby. He'd never been great at the game but made the first team on and off. Of the four brothers in the family who had attended Blackrock he'd been the only one not to win a prize for something or other. One of them had won a gold medal, for an essay on Hamlet. Maybe my own prize has been to outlive them all he thought and then blessed himself.

This evening the game was to be played at Doctor Cooke's house. For the previous two weeks Sergeant Reilly had won and he had intimated to Bill Finan on the Saturday night that he was on a "bit of a roll." Bill Finan grinned and made some smart comment about the late-night bar extension for the festival being a certainty. The festival was held each August for a week. All the young people organised their holidays around it and came back from Boston or London.

Kevin Fahy closed the shop at one o'clock and went home to his dinner. As on every Wednesday; the smell of roast beef met him at the gate. He walked up the three steps to the path and then around by the side of the house and wiped his feet on the mat before turning the brass knob into the scullery. His wife was loading the dishwasher.

"Did you have a good day?"

"Fairly quiet."

"Anyone strange in?"

"No, nobody strange. Oh Mrs. Lynskey called in and said John will be home for the festival and he'll mend the lawnmower."

"That's great, your dinner's on the table."

He turned on the radio to get the headlines. Something about the farmers marching against turnip prices, a ship capsizing off the Greek Coast – everybody rescued, and the inevitable condemnations by someone about some tragedy or other in the North. He switched the dial, watching the counter run from left to right. A lady with a cultured English accent said "And now over to our Essex studio for Gardening World. This week; how to detect slugs."

"I think I'll switch it off," Kevin said to his wife.

"Okay. Would you like a sherry?"

It was four o'clock in the barracks and Sergeant Reilly was bored. The only thing he'd done all day was read the paper and answer the phone. In the afternoon things were usually quiet. It appeared to him that any problems which required his attention always arose in the evenings after he'd closed up the barracks. In his absence a Green Man switch on the front door connected visitors by radio with the Garda station in Tuam but people rarely used that service. Some mornings were made up of a series of complaints to him about things which had happened the previous night.

"I locked the gate and there's no way the bull could have escaped."

"It ate all of my cabbages."

"Mrs. Moriarty is a liar, I'm sorry Guard, I hate to say it but she is."

Somebody had phoned to ask about a provisional driving licence. He remembered a sick joke about a man being asked to produce his licence to terrorists before being made to drive a proxy bomb into an army roadblock. He tackled the crossword again before putting on the kettle, setting himself a target of three more words before coffee.

At about half-past five it began to rain, pelting down on the village, running from the gutters into the streets. An old lady sheltered in the doorway of Lennon's Hardware shop on Bridge Street. Then, almost as suddenly as it had begun, the rain stopped. The sky cleared and the heat of the evening sun turned the puddles into steam which rose like theatrical smoke from the tarmac square in the middle of the village. The doors of almost every house opened and children, under orders to be home in time for tea, tumbled out into the streets chasing footballs and tricycles. Doctor Cooke glanced at his watch. He was looking forward to tonight's game. He always felt it a luxury not to have to move out of the house every third Wednesday. Win, lose or draw, he liked only having to go upstairs when the evening's play had ended. He had slipped on ice crossing the square and broken his left hip going to the barracks one cold night about five years previously and treasured his home games all the more after that.

His wife and he had spent the previous weekend in Enniscrone. Their son Michael had a small summer cottage there and had given them a spare set of keys;

"Drop in whenever you feel like it and keep an eye on the place."

He recalled the long white beach with the castle-shaped seaweed baths at the bottom of the cliff. He'd seen it advertised for sale in a paper a couple of days later as a dwelling house in need of "some internal repairs." The place was ruined inside, self respecting pigs would turn their snouts up at it he thought. A rather flattering photograph and a dose of small print would steer the property in the direction of some romantic foreigner with more money than sense. Still, they'd enjoyed the weekend. A long stroll on the beach before lunch on Sunday and then a leisurely drive back through south Mayo. He wondered how the Galway minor hurlers would get on the following Sunday and made a mental note not to miss the match if it was on the television.

The clouds gathered again over Castletown and Sergeant Reilly put on his greatcoat as he prepared to leave. He locked the door which led from the house into the station and flicked through the local paper which had been delivered sometime that afternoon. He turned to the Court Diary to see was his name mentioned. It wasn't.

"I'll put the dog into the shed when I get back!" he shouted to his wife who was upstairs somewhere. She appeared on the landing with a pile of blankets in her arms.

"Oh you're off are you? Best of luck tonight and don't forget to put the dog in the shed when you get back!"

He mumbled to himself and pulled the door after him. He went out the gate and turned right stopping to buy tobacco in Julia's Corner Shop. The H.B. freezer was humming and Julia emerged from the sitting room behind the shop to serve him.

Kevin Fahy was about fifty yards from Dr. Cooke's house when Sergeant Reilly came around the corner having taken the shortcut through the lane that ran behind the school.

"How are you feeling tonight John?" he asked.

"Lucky Kevin, very lucky."

"So Bill Finan's extension is in the bag if you win?"

"I'll tell you Kevin, I'd nearly get him a dancing licence if I make it three in a row. How's herself?"

"Oh not a bother on her, and Mary?"

"Grand. Grand."

They reached the house and rang the doorbell. It was opened by Mrs. Cooke. "Come in, Father Mitchell is inside."

The church bell clanged as the Chemist and the Sergeant hung their coats under Doctor Cooke's stairs for the very last time.

A Matter of Credibility

~

H. D. Guillamore was a very important person. He was important at home in the bosom of his family. He was important in the small village in County Meath where his father had been the last member of the Guillamore clan to have a seat in the House of Lords. He was important too in his solicitor's practice in the once-grand offices of "Guillamore and O'Grady" exactly halfway between Blackhall Place and the Four Courts. Most of those dusty contexts in which he was important had somehow become ever so slightly less important, but where he was still undeniably important (and perhaps even a little more so now) was in the glamorous setting of the Refugee Appeals' Tribunal just off the unglamorous docks in the heart of Dublin City.

47

Fridays were the worst because the traffic out of the city began earlier than usual. Unless he got away before four in the afternoon he'd be stuck on the Navan Road for hours. Bumper to bumper. The two o'clock case would determine the outcome of the traffic dilemma, because if it ran over the allocated hour then the second case would almost certainly make him late in leaving. On a chilly Friday evening in October he glanced at the clock on the wall and it was a quarter past three. On his right the Applicant, a Moldovan national, was still being cross-examined by the Presenting Officer. The interpreter was a pretty, older lady, who smiled courteously at him each time their eyes met.

'Is the railway station thirty kilometres away or thirty minutes away?' the Presenting Officer asked for clarification. H.D. looked down at his notes and saw that he'd stopped moving his hand so it was now apparent he'd given up taking an account of the hearing. In truth there had been a clear conflict between the answers given on the original questionnaire and the interview conducted some weeks later. In one the Applicant said she was a hairdresser, and had her own salon in her house, however the other state-ment had her claiming that the salon was across the road from her house but that she owned the building in which it was situated. She was only a few weeks away from re-entering the hair-cutting market in Moldova whichever version she now wanted to stand over. He heard words he did not understand, then the interpreter spoke,

'She says that the railway station is in a town which is twenty or so kilometres away.'

H.D. looked at the Applicant without malice or pity. He began to write again and scribbled *"Answer re railway station now revised downwards by a third!!!"* He saw the file of the next case peeping out from the pile on the desk and waited for the evidence to finish.

It was twenty-one and a half minutes to four when the next Applicant began to tell of the woe and hardship experienced by him against the backdrop of chaos and political revolution in a central African country where the civil war had lasted nearly twelve years. H.D. listened with some interest to the description of pitched battles fought on narrow streets and of how families of one tribe loyal to the former dictator bundled their lives into suitcases and sprinted through the warm, damp blood of neighbours butchered moments earlier. He felt the moment approach however, as he did in every case, when the true test of the veracity of the story would occur. Sometimes it was a discrepancy in the accounts given during the long application process or an embellishment of some incident which was introduced in the hearing for effect. Sometimes it was an exercise of painting into a corner where answer after answer led to the cul-de-sac of lies where they were eventually left with absolutely no escape. There was the jaded ubiquitous tale of a generous benefactor called "John" who provided a false passport and free passage by plane via unknown countries to Dublin Airport and then disappeared taking the passport with him. Sometimes, rarely though, it was an admission of falsehood by the Applicant themselves.

'What was the address of your parents' house?' the P.O. asked.

'Twenty three Mode Street,' the Applicant replied in near-perfect English. The Presenting Officer's face betrayed the slightest hue of triumph as she closed in for the kill.

'But on your application form you list their address as *thirty four* Mode Street?' She looked at H.D. Guillamore and as she made the accusation he made a note *"Number of parents' house different in oral evidence!!!!"*

'My cousin lived there, that is where we lived after our house was destroyed.'

Guillamore felt the moment gush up at him out of the file like forgotten money-notes found in an old book.

'Is your cousin going to give evidence?' H.D. taunted the Applicant.

'No Sir. My cousin cannot give evidence because he is dead.'

H.D. made his own notes and waited for the Presenting Officer to press home the advantage. When she did not he glanced again at the clock and took matters into his own hands.

'Is there anybody apart from yourself who can give evidence of the alleged persecution you say you suffered?'

In the four years of hearing refugee cases he recalled no more than three applicants who had produced witnesses. Mostly they had no need to, as they would only be providing ammunition for the exposure of even more glaring discrepancies in their already well-perforated testimony. The Applicant paused for a moment and took off his glasses and wiped an apparent tear from his eye,

'Yes Sir, most certainly definitely. My friend Ezekiel Tundele is waiting outside and would be most wishful of giving more evidence Sir.'

H.D. Guillamore's heart sank like an Easter-egg made of granite. The bloody last thing he wanted was to be here until God-knows-how late listening to some trumped-up corroborating fable from another unmeritorious source. The solicitor for the Applicant was a man H.D. had never particularly liked and he now made to get to his feet to go and fetch the star witness. A crossbow bolt from the Presenting Officer hit him between the eyes,

'The Tribunal should know that we were never told in advance that there would be any other witnesses. On the notification form they were asked to tick the box and send it back if there *were* any.'

'Do you object to the witness being called, Miss Freelander?' H.D. lobbed the ball attractively for her to smash home.

'We were never notified,' Miss Freelander obliged.

'I'm afraid I can't allow any witnesses to be called if they're not notified in advance to the Presenting Officer. It's a matter of credibility really. There must be *some* formality to these hearings.' H.D. shrugged his shoulders in a gesture which washed his hands of the matter. The hearing concluded a short time later and, as H.D. Guillamore took the elevator to the underground car park, he knew that he would be home on time. He'd noticed the witness outside the room as he left; a young black man with only one hand. H.D. wondered what had convinced him to attend and be prepared to perjure himself. Perhaps "perjure" was the wrong word, because of course they didn't take the oath, but whatever the equivalent in their culture would be. He made a mental note to get one of the researchers to find out what it might be in that part of Africa. He imagined it would turn out to be some pledge to deliver up so many goats per untruth, or something like that.

The following year, H.D. Guillamore was re-appointed for another term as a member of the R.A.T. He revelled in this new boost to his confidence and looked proudly over his shoulder at years of important and valuable public service which had now been rewarded by an extension of tenure. He sat in the glamorous building and drank coffee and looked out the window at the developing dockland and thought of himself as a type of zookeeper restricting the number of visitors to the enclosure of the Celtic Tiger.

In late July, as the sun ensured the temperature was enjoyable in the evening, H.D. eased into fifth gear and gobbled up the road beyond Dunshaughlin. He failed to see the small dog chasing a football until it was too late. His expensive Scandinavian motor-car took the brunt of the impact against the gable-end of a derelict cottage. The air-bag exploded into his face.

In the corner of a pub in the dockland area some months later, a man with only one hand watched as his pint settled. His colleague was a kindly carpenter who had employed him on a cash basis to help him make ends meet while his family were still within the asylum process awaiting a decision on their future.

'You were on the scene just after the accident happened?'

'Yes, I went out to see if there was anything I could do of course.'

'And what happened then?'

'The guy in the Saab asked me to put my hand down into the pocket of the door to get his inhaler. He said he needed a few puffs or else he would die.'

'But you couldn't reach it?'

'No, no I couldn't. After all that had happened I just wasn't able to help him.'

Dixton Larkin Writhes Again

~

Dixton Larkin was dying for a pee. He'd been sent by his great benefactor, and surrogate parent, Aunt Sheila, on an errand out into the wild countryside of County Meath to collect a box of 500 sets of rosary beads bought by her over the phone as a result of an ad in Buy and Sell. Dixton's only interest in that yellow publication were the personal adverts at the back where blonde widows from Moscow, with legs up to their armpits, sought *"Kind professional man with own car and house for everlasting love"* (and perhaps citizenship). He'd picked up the beads from a farmer in Trim (the town, not the physical condition) and had handed over the agreed swap value; one copy of "The Pope's Visit"-the album" and a handful of miraculous medals which were rumoured to have been owned at one stage by Dana. His aunt had an eye for a bargain. Dixton hoped that the removal from her collection of the Vatican Vinyl would ensure for him a future of Saturday morning lie-ins free from the caterwauling strains of "He's got the whole world in his hands" sung by a gazillion teenagers in the rain on a racecourse.

Thinking about the rain reminded him of his urinary dilemma and he strained his eyes through the windscreen looking for a suitable place in which to gain relief. Up ahead he saw the unmistakable neat spire of a Church of Ireland church and he began to ready himself to stop there and sneak around behind it to do the needful. His aunt was unrelenting on the subject of the "other" crowd.

"They're protesting against us Dixton. That's why they're called Protestants. Make no mistake, there's never been an itch made that the Devil couldn't scratch."

Dixton rarely engaged with his aunt when the subject of religion was raised, as his bed and board in Ailesbury Crescent were largely dependant on his ability to weather the storms of religious fervour whipped up by her from time to time. He had no real desire to imperil his position there in that regard as his first year in practice at the Irish Bar had not as yet yielded a single sign of any wealth to come.

He was at bursting-point when he pulled his aunt's car in to the grassy lay-bye outside the church. Abandoning his keys in the ignition for much lower ideals he clambered out of the car and scrambled up the path into the churchyard, exercising what he feared might be the very last of his canal-work control. He managed to make it around to the part of the property shielded from view of the road by the chapel itself and, with his relief, startled the afternoon nap of some nettles and dock-leaves growing remarkably peacefully side by side. As he began to walk round the other way to complete a full circle he saw a freshly-dug grave yawning up at the sky and a roll of fake-grass carpet lolling to one side on the mound of clay. As he always did, when Death or the hint of it crossed his path, he thought of his aunt. The sound of engines from the roadway interrupted his daydream and he continued on his way but was met with the sight of four men carrying a coffin on their shoulders in sombre step up the path at him preceded by a vicar in full robes. Dixton stepped to one side to let them pass.

There were quite a few mourners following the coffin and for the most part they appeared to be in their seventies or even older. The exception to this age-profile was a small good-looking lady in perhaps her early thirties who wore a large black brimmed hat with a lacy type arrangement drooping from its edges. Dixton was struck by her some-what sexy demeanour given the circumstances. She glanced his way as she drew level with him and he gave her what he hoped would be interpreted as a sympathetic smile rather than a lecherous grin. She smiled back.

After the funeral party had passed by Dixton stepped out onto the path again and was about to head back to the car when a man carrying a wreath came in through the gate and hurried up the incline.

"Are you here for the funeral?" he asked Dixton.

"No, no," Dixton faltered. "I just dropped in to visit one of the graves." He lied lyingly.

"This one?" the man pointed to the huge granite headstone at the head of the plot Dixton's right foot was standing on.

"Yes," he nodded sadly. "This one. Just passing by and well…"

"Victor Pardue," the man read the name on the grave. "I knew him from the Select Vestry meetings. An absolute tragedy the way it happened eh?"

"I try not to dwell on it too much," Dixton said bravely and then made to step around the wreath-man.

"Then you must have known poor old Louise?" the man nodded in the direction of the burial occurring some two dozen yards away.

"No," Dixton replied. "No I didn't. Sorry, I've got to go now." He made another attempt to proceed but old flowery was having none of it.

"Hold this," the man ordered as he foisted the wreath on Dixton. "I know I've got it here somewhere. Now where *are* my glasses?"

Dixton could begin to feel the other brand of bodily function stirring within him. He thought about dumping the wreath and legging it but decided for some ridiculous reason not to. The man found his glasses and put them on. He struggled to pull a piece of paper out of his jacket pocket. It was an Order of Service. The man smiled helpfully and unfolded the paper.

"Ah yes," he announced triumphantly. "Lottie Maybury, Louise's sister, was married to Victor's brother Frank. So you see… "

A much louder clearing of the throat than usual hawked up at them from the graveside ceremony and the man pointed over Dixton's shoulder.

"They need the wreath now. I wonder if you'd be kind enough to carry it for me while I sort out my glasses?"

"Of course," Dixton croaked, inhaling some of the pollen from the flowers and turning with the man to attend Louise's last farewell.

Two hours later Dixton was nursing his fifth cup of tea and being bored to tears by an old lady who insisted on telling him her life's story.

"We lived in the Rectory in Tullamore before the war so you see we're really from…"

"Tullamore?" Dixton offered.

"How did you guess?" she asked, shaking her head in admiration at this dazzling display of perception. Dixton looked around the gathering and wondered how he was going to extract himself from it. He'd been press-ganged into driving three people back to the home of the deceased after the burial. This was to allow the hearse to get on some-where else to continue remaindering or whatever they called it. Once inside the house, a rambling manor on the edge of the Boyne valley, it had been a relentless torrent of reminiscences about Louise's triumphs with turnips and marrows at agricultural shows.

"Everybody loved her turnips. She even grew one in the shape of a cat once, she said it wasn't deliberate but of course nobody knew the habits of turnips like Louise did."

Dixton was bored to death and really wanted to be somewhere else watching paint dry or counting loose chippings on the Clonee by-pass. The old dear from Tullamore was now off on the subject of bran-flakes as a meat substitute on the Atkins Diet. Dixton saw his chance as a tray of bits of salmon on bits of brown bread made its way towards them being held acrobatically over her head by the pretty lady he'd seen at the churchyard.

"Let me," he offered as he stood up and lunged towards her with an offer to relieve her of the tray. She smiled in an expression loaded with gratitude and possibilities.

"Thank you so much, it's nice to know that gentlemen still exist."

Dixton began his journey for the door into the hall and edged his way across the thronged room. As he stepped into the carpeted corridor a voice stopped him in his tracks.

"Ah there he is. Lottie, this is the young chap I was telling you about, the one who knew Victor."

Dixton could feel things closing in around him as he turned to face a dear lady in her sixties and the man who'd thrust the wreath at him. She was clearly gearing up for an old chat about Victor and Frank and all those other dead people Dixton didn't know at all. She stepped forward and held out her hand. Dixton fended her off with the tray and then side-stepped both of them and said,

"Excuse me for a moment, I need to find a bathroom."

"Straight up the stairs, second on the left," said the man with a slightly puzzled look on his face. "We'll wait here for you shall we?"

As Dixton bolted upstairs, still carrying the tray, he heard the old dear say,

"I *am* looking forward to speaking with that young man. Victor had *so* few friends you know. I wonder if he worked in the abattoir as well."

The bathroom door was locked and Dixton began to wonder how on earth he was going to extricate himself from this ghastly situation which had really not been of his own making (apart from that fib about visiting the grave of course). He saw that one of the bedroom doors was open and as the coast was clear he peeked in and spotted a window leading onto a small balcony. He closed the bedroom door behind him as he entered and looked about for a suitable place to abandon the tray. He wolfed the last of the food from it and put it down on a dressing table. The window was one of those modern ones which opens a couple of different ways and Dixton struggled with the chrome handle trying to get it into the position most favourable for his escape. As he did so he heard a toilet flush. It seemed much closer than the bathroom which had been locked. What he'd thought was a wardrobe was an en-suite bathroom door and as it opened he nipped in behind it and hoped he wouldn't be spotted.

The pretty lady from whom he'd rescued the tray stepped into the middle of the room. She walked to a chest of drawers and began to unzip her dress as she rooted with her free hand in one of the drawers. In the mirror over the dressing table she caught sight of Dixton sandwiched between the door and the wall.

"What on earth are you doing in my room?" she screamed. Dixton did not really feel up to explaining and so he made a dash for the window.

"Harry, Heather, come quickly, there's a burglar in my bedroom!" the lady shouted to the people downstairs while Dixton got wedged in the window. The next thing he felt was the almighty thwack of the tray on his rear-end as the owner of the bedroom struck a few blows for constitutional property rights. Dixton was assisted out onto the balcony by this attack and, as he hung from the plaster surround by his hands and before he could ascertain the scale of the drop, he heard more voices in the bedroom he'd just abandoned. He let go. The electric-blue Porsche broke his fall. And his collar-bone.

At the end of November Dixton accompanied his Master to a consultation in one of the rooms in the base-ment of the Four Courts. Dixton had read the brief and so he walked, as all Devils should, some paces behind his mentor carrying case-books and photocopied precedents from the Irish Reports. It was a complex case about the adjustment of pension rights but it seemed that there was every chance that the case might settle.

As he approached the consultation room Dixton's gown caught on a fire-extinguisher and he dropped his pile of books and papers. He went down onto his hands and knees to retrieve them and as he did he heard a familiar voice from the room wending its way out to him in the corridor.

"When all of this is over I'd like you to give me some advice about my grandmother's estate if you have time."

"I'd be delighted to," Dixton's Master replied. There was a lull for a second and then the instructing solicitor, Mr Burke, spoke next.

"Have the Gardai had any luck tracking down that maniac who tried to steal the tray at her funeral?"

"No," the lady replied. "But I'd definitely recognise him if I ever saw him on Crime Line or any of those programmes. He caused four thousand euros worth of damage to Heather's car. Imagine conning your way into a funeral just to steal a brass tray!"

"He'll show up somewhere, someday," the solicitor consoled.

Dixton Larkin was already on his way to showing up on the back page of Buy and Sell in an ad which read;

> *Qualified barrister seeks part-time work in Siberia selling second-hand rosary beads. Speaks Leaving-cert standard Irish and loves salmon on brown bread. No reasonable offer refused!*

The Voyager

~

On the way to Tokyo the train from the airport passed by thousands of misshapen buildings which housed the workers and doctors and shopkeepers and little-known painters who made up suburban numbers. Block after block of apartments squared the horizon in an odd way as the carriage lurched on a bend and he stretched out a hand to stop his rucksack from falling from an adjacent chair. It was an unnecessary act on his part. The seats were like giant dentists' chairs and turned on a plate at the push of a pedal. He imagined how dramatic it would be, during an argument on the train with a companion, to suddenly swivel away out of the row. It would require pushing the pedal with your hand but he had already forgotten how much pressure was needed with your foot to do the trick and the sequence of thoughts which had led to the theory dissipated inside his new distraction; a body lying in a rice field.

It was unclear whether it had been male or female but the corpse or sleeper (and he thought the latter unlikely) seemed to have been overtaken more slowly by the train than the rest of the countryside had been. Perhaps he'd been mistaken about the speed, but he had no doubt about what he'd seen. It jolted his easy noticing and hauled him back through some sort of intellectual loop to a point at which he was forced to think about why he'd come back to Japan. He imagined violence leading to the scene in the field but knew that it was more likely to be an ordinary death, heart giving up or lungs giving in, rather than the heavy forced endings of feud or fight. He wondered if he should tell someone, raise the alarm, be the messenger, stop the train. What would that achieve? It would be next to impossible to tell the story unless he found someone who spoke his language. What then? How could he pinpoint the place? The train was now miles past the scene and he could not even say how many. What would it prevent, his telling the world about the thing that he'd seen in the rice? Nothing except perhaps the early decay of the body. Even that was un-certain as he did not know how long the body had been there or if he had been the only person to notice it. For all he knew the ambulance could already be on its way. Wouldn't someone have stayed with the body to await the arrival of the medics? Not if they'd been on their own and had left to telephone for help. Supposing the body were only sleeping, drunk perhaps or tired? What then? Well then the ambulance could take its time or not bother arriving at all.

Each apartment balcony bore the scar of air conditioning; the ventilator motor. Like giant transistor radios they hung about outside while their good-looking control panels on the inside of each dwelling brought warmth or cold at the caress of a button. The ticket man passed through the carriage and in his demeanour epitomised the calm workings of this entire country which the voyager had first experienced only eighteen months earlier. That trip had been a once-in-a-lifetime holiday to the greatest soccer tournament in the world. Then he'd been drawn here with thousands of other supporters from dozens of other countries to wear his national football shirt and paint his face and scream the daylights out of his vocal chords. He remembered the matches, the euphoria of the goals, the depressions fostered by opponents' successes and the pride and power of milling with thousands of like-minded men and women who'd also mortgaged houses or sweet-talked bank managers to make the trip. Like one huge coloured tortoise they'd moved to Tokyo, Niigata, Ibaraki and Yokohama and on to a penalty shoot-out in Korea against the mighty Spanish. A lifetime's worth of emotion in three weeks at the mercy of a leather ball and complete chance. "Konbanwa"; good evening, the word came to mind for no reason, it was morning in Japan and Tokyo waited down the track with its sushi bars opened wide in welcome.

He reserved a seat on the bullet train to Niigata for later that afternoon and determined in the intervening time to

67

visit some of the places he'd seen on his first trip. It was a decision he'd only made after seeing the train time-table and he wondered if somehow this spontaneity spoiled or tainted the trip. Shouldn't everything have been carefully planned in every detail and followed to the letter? No, it shouldn't. Predictability was the chicken pox of enjoyment. Enjoyment? He stopped in a small café in Tokyo station and had coffee and some dried sweet biscuits. This was where they'd snacked on his first trip and it only dawned on him as he paid the check and prepared to leave. Almost like a sign, this unexpected carbon of previous actions confirmed his decision to visit the past before he boarded the train to Niigata.

Roppongi. This was where hookers and strippers were not outcasts. No moral judgements here; just money changing hands and bodies changing clothes. The callers on the street, men from Ghana and Senegal, competed with each other in a battle fought by flyers and one-liners for the money paid by businessmen to have more than their egos massaged. Even now, in daylight, the trade was only just the slow side of brisk. Print blue silhouettes of cross-legged girls wooed in the punters with a whiff of neon. Outside each 'entertainment centre' the people-watchers pounced on the wallets of the lonely. This theatre of love-exchanges was the repository of a hundred thousand desires a day, desires so hot they put the sun in the shade.

He turned corners and recognised places he'd forgotten he'd ever been. Some half-baked man in a flashy white suit propositioned him and he laughed so hard he had to stop to catch his breath. It was not clear whether the man was offering his own services or those of a principal, but it didn't matter. He stopped at a stand which sold dumplings. The fifty-yen coin, with the hole in the middle, flashed out of his hand like a glimpse of that other time. He imagined a newly minted pile of them wrapped in treasury brown paper. If he poked a hole at each end through the paper he'd have a telescope. Two rolls for binoculars. The dream never ended as long as the dreamer kept putting the coins in the slot. Roppongi. Left there by ten to three on a church clock no-one ever looked at. He remembered the body in the field.

That afternoon at exactly 3.11 the Shiknansen left Tokyo Central with the reserved carriages full and satisfied. The train swished its way through the suburbs past the Saitama Indoor Arena and the multiplicity of Sony and Toshiba signs which the skyscrapers wore like headbands. As the countryside appeared on either side of the tracks the train bullied its way across the width of Japan like a giant zip on wheels, joining or dividing depending on the way you wanted to see the teeth. For a while he slept and when he awoke it was precisely one half way through the journey. He thought in depth for the first time about his friend and travelling companion at the World Cup; Billy Field.

They'd met in college ten years earlier in an old English university where the divisions they would have faced in Ireland at that time were invisible. Protestant, Catholic, Unionist, Loyalist, Republican, Taig; these were home-made tags which carried pride and hatred in equal measure in mirror image. He and Field had simply been friends.

69

They'd shared the intimacy of that frozen time which is university life. They'd endured the penury and mischief of student days which moulds boys into grown-up boys and they'd watched each other fail and triumph with women far too good and bad for them.

Back home the voyager's grown-up life waited for him now. His wife and two children had seen him to the airport. An office in Dublin held his papers and future, like a giant maiden aunt dispensing largesse and security in rations which straddled the tax year. Cases sat in envelopes waiting to be won and lost and the real thrill was that you never knew in advance. Paid well to call people liars under the umbrella of absolute privilege, where would you get it? He drank from his water bottle and smiled.

Niigata; the big town with awfully little to say for itself. Here his countrymen had come from one-nil down to draw with the holders of the African Nations' Cup. He and Field had stayed up all night after the match and given their hotel room to two fans who had nowhere to stay. It was an act of pragmatism more than kindness as they'd already decided to return to the island where they'd spent the two nights before the game. At least *Field* had decided and then the voyager had agreed to go with him rather than strike out for Okinawa on his own. That had been their original plan, to go there between the first two games. The chance to taste history, and meet GI's in snack bars built in the shadow of the Midway, had gone and yet he hadn't been too disappointed. To witness Field in love was a far greater novelty. Field had met and fallen for a bouncy, pretty, clever girl whose mum ran a bar on Sado Island. Her name was Yuki (pronounced 'you-key') and she'd arrived into Billy Field's life like a freight train loaded with possibility and comfort.

On the ferry to the island he remembered their first trip on this same boat. The sun had shone for most of the journey but when they arrived in Ryotsu port the sky had dimmed. They came from an island themselves and perhaps that was why they'd chosen Sado-Ga-Shima as a base for the first match. It was a peculiar place with a naïve twist to its people which rendered them a very different lot from the people of Honshu or any other part of Japan he'd read about, met or seen. They kept almost to themselves, if that makes sense. They'd let you in a little to their lives and befriend you and help you but it was very hard sometimes to know how far you'd been accepted. Subsequent meetings could, by the hazard, either reveal enormous progress or regression in the process of the friendship. In that way they were not unlike the Irish. Billy Field became addicted to this uncertainty and for a guy whose normal E.T.A. with women was thirty five or forty minutes after check in, the complete stone-walling by Yuki in their initial meeting had convinced him to extend his holiday beyond the World Cup. He'd lingered in the bar until he had to be noticed and once noticed he stayed in the way until conversation was inevitable. The journey from speech to shared breakfasts was considerably longer, he'd since confided.

Back home Billy made plausible excuses for his extended stay. He told of storms and non-refundable plane tickets and ferries that wouldn't sail and phones that couldn't be used to call Europe and a hat-full of other fibs. He severed the latest commitment in Belfast months later when the moment was right and became properly single. Yuki came to visit for New Year and the rest was cinema seats and constant e-mail. The voyager had been stunned and delighted by the innocence and the honesty and the purity of it all. Billy Field went from serial monogamist to star-struck teenager in a matter of less than a week and all it had taken was a couple of songs by Toto on a karaoke machine and, of course, the right girl.

The wedding took place just one week short of a year since their first meeting. In a ceremony in a temple shaded by enormous pine trees, surrounded by close friends and annoying incense, Billy Field and Yuki Ito exchanged rings and in a mix of East meets West, satisfied both families. The CD player beside the lacquered water bowls played "Africa" and then they repaired to a tiny restaurant in Mano for a meal and a late night. Billy was a fabulous golfer and the morning after the wedding the two of them played nine holes as they'd done a year earlier. The scores didn't matter, but what was different was that Billy was now a part of Sado Island. He'd married a local girl and, although she'd agreed to come and live in Ireland, this island would be a part of his life now forever for at least a month or six weeks each Summer. That was the deal.

And now the voyager had come to his destination. A small local bus from the ferry took him to the village of Mano. He passed the small supermarket where he'd discovered yoghurt butterscotch and eaten a whole packet in the car park and then returned instantly to buy some more. He got off the bus outside the post office and began the steep climb up the road past the temple to the golf course. He stepped over a foot-high electric fence between a field of cows and the seventh fairway. It was nine-thirty now and the evening was drawing in and the course was deserted. Up the hill towards the green he walked and felt the strain of the day in the backs of his legs. He reached the inch-high rough to the rear of the green and then turned to his left towards the path leading to the next tee. He saw it now; a gold statue of Buddha rising out of the forest floor and looking to the hills on the other side of Mano Bay. The only sound was the shuffle of wind through the leaves on the branches and the chuckle of water trickling down the smooth stone into the small pool surrounding the earth island on which the statue stood. He swung his ruck-sack from his back and lowered it to the ground. From one of the zipped side-pockets, he took a leather bag. He remembered the train tracks as the zip hissed at him.

He scattered half of Billy Field's ashes into the pond as directed in the Will and then took a small trowel from his belongings and (removing his socks and shoes first) walked into the middle of the seventh green. Carefully he dug a small square sod out and laid it to one side. He scooped four small trowel loads of earth and threw three of them into the pond. The last he left on the trowel and, when he'd poured the remainder of the ashes, he placed this earth on top before replacing the sod. He filled his water bottle from the pond twice and dampened the square he'd replaced. Again, Billy had specified this in his instructions.

Finally he took a cigarette lighter from his pocket. It was a cheap model with the name of Yuki's mother's bar on the side in Japanese lettering. He lit the leather bag by stuffing it with paper and turning it upside down to shield it from the wind. When it was lighting properly he threw it across the small pond to the feet of the gold statue. He didn't think the bag would burn but it did as it landed on its side so that the paper had plenty of air to fuel it.

As he walked back down the hill it began to rain and the raindrops mixed with his tears and ran down his cheeks and onto his shirt to where a tiny speck of ash now caused a stain to appear between his shirt pocket and second button. Somewhere in Ireland Billy's car was in a junkyard. Somewhere on Sado-Ga-Shima Yuki's family was still waiting for her body to be released from Narita Airport morgue. A sunny winter's day when it appeared safe to overtake on a bend had not really been sunny or safe at all. The voyager remembered the body he'd seen lying in a rice field that morning and suddenly the combination of the words 'field' and 'body' was too much and he sat down. He leaned against a tree until his rucksack cut into his back and he began to imagine that everything was all right and that he was crying for some other reason.

Monday July 2nd 1973

~

"SOLDIER SHOT DEAD; 47 PEOPLE INJURED IN UDA BOMBING."

Nothing made sense that day with the rain pelting down on the corrugated-iron roof of the studio behind her mother's house in Drumcondra. The water raced down the slant onto the edge to where there should have been a gutter but wasn't. Like theories etched with biros onto pages and then abandoned into canvas holdalls (which were in turn discarded under stairs) the raindrops left their mark and then they too disappeared onto the grass where irrelevance lay in wait. It hammered like nails overhead while Catherine Ellis tried to mould green plasticine into the shape of a stranger's face. She never knew her subject in advance, all she did was work her way up to an encounter as soon as the mouth eyes ears appeared. One time the face looked like hers until she took hold of the situation and gave the ghoul a third ear, under the chin.

"How multifarious your ears are Granny." "All the better to hear myself think my dear child."

All around the studio the tools of her pursuit lay like relatives dozing at a wedding late on, ready to be revived and led back to the dance floor to take centre, to be applied and to revel and reveal as the wood or other material was wearied down into something recognizable. Her hands stretched out away from her for an instant giving the figure a moment to itself in mid-birth like a rest the midwives want themselves. Outside the rain was relentless and she wondered for a second whether in fact it might not soak away after all but build up drop upon drop like a wall, one drop overlapping every two, until it had her surrounded in the shed. That word sounded so unappealing, 'shed', surely she meant studio or workshop? Nope. Shed it was and like a flash the rain stopped and she missed the comfort of its threat like a punch pulled in mid air.

"LIBERIAN TANKER ON FIRE".

"Please don't insult my intelligence Catherine. Or your own. There are two things happening here and you're in control of both of them. First there's you there with your inherited anger making you unreasonable and then there's the situation that the other you has created with me where I'm being ignored on one level and accused on another, both simultaneously. Do you accept that? Can we back it up a few steps and talk about the real us for a moment? Can we do that, can we?"

Sculptures lurked in the immediate background. Unsaleable, unsold, unselling. They marked the parameters of ambition in clay and wood and mixed media. Nobody was going to see them there and yet she wondered if that were not the very result she wanted. Could she be out front in some small space in the middle of town standing over her work while people she vaguely knew made up their own minds? It's all about knowing what you like. Like wine and love really. Don't have to shop expensive just find the thing that makes you less sad than the other things on offer. Simple as pie. She made an apple pie once and had it out of the oven hot and ready and vanilla ice-cream on the side but it went cold and when it finally got eaten the good had gone out of it and her both.

FROM TODAY DUBLIN'S 5 MAIN COAL MERCHANTS WILL BE KNOWN AS COAL DISTRIBUTORS LIMITED.

More depth in the eyes she pushed and made the pupils stand out a little less and they evinced an air of learning simply by moving back slightly. If only it were that simple. Steam rose now from the tarmac path up to the back door as the weather which had booked its two weeks in July made a comeback. Unexpected sunshine is less welcome than unexpected rain she thought. People want to plan ahead and be right; no-one much cares about spontaneity going wrong, it's just the way of the world really. For a moment it began to rain again on the roof but it was either frightened away by the sun or it might have been drops from a tree.

Out beyond the terrace of houses and their inhabitants Dublin lay in waiting. It was a maelstrom of opportunities, grabbed, missed and disappointing. Interviews went wrong and candidates never realized a thing and bussed home to mammy with their fingers crossed. Away from her studio shed whole, other, fulfilled lives were being lived out by people she may have even sat beside at one stage in Clery's shoe department or at a pantomime in the Gaiety theatre. Somewhere in the claptrapness of it all, young, new, enthusiastic lovers lay sweating side by side with the peace that follows pleasure. Dogs panted after each other and tractors made the very odd and occasional appearance at the fringes of this city; peeping over hedges from ploughed fields which were soon to become housing estates.

FORT WORTH FIVE UNJUSTLY IMPRISONED, SAYS BISHOP.

"I'm trapped in this bloody marriage Monsignor, what's the bishop going to do about *that*.?"

"Please Mrs. Ryan…"

"My name is Ellis not Ryan, that's *his* name."

"Please Mrs. Ryan, you have to understand that the whole process of investigation is careful and measured and cannot be rushed in the way in which civil decrees of divorce are granted by the courts in Protestant countries."

"I know but surely the interviews and all the paperwork gave a very clear picture?"

"I must ask you Mrs. Ryan to be patient with us as we have been with you. There is a very long way to go before we would even be in a position to send this case forward for a decision."

A short distance away from her mother's house the Archbishop's Palace was surrounded by a high wall and heavy iron gates. She wondered if they'd throw the decision over the wall at her or allow her pick it up at the gate. A thought struck her that as her decision might be imprisoned behind the walls of the Bishop's palace so too was a body imprisoned in a coffin and the hearse was a bit like a prison van making the journey from court to jail. Of course the hearse was always empty on the return leg of that trip. "Sorry for your troubles," people said in Ireland when they sympathized with relatives at a funeral. She remembered her father's funeral with the cold white walls of Fanagan's Funeral Home like the cricket screens on the pitch at Trinity College in the middle of June. A frail condensed version of herself in mourning while people she never knew shook her hand and were sorry for her troubles. It was an assault on her whole world to be whipped out of school in the middle of Home Economics to be told that there had been an accident.

"Finn Ellis was a good man. A good father, a good husband and a good friend to everyone who knew him. I remember one sunny Friday evening about three months ago when I met him out walking his dog by the canal behind Croke Park…"

"Tipperary 5–4 (19) overwhelm Cork 1–10 (13) in astonishing rally".

Brandy was in the air after the funeral. Home to sandwiches and ham and cold chicken and the slurp of Guinness from the bottle. Catherine gathered up papers from the floor of the studio and bundled them together into a box which held a few bits of rubbish already. She turned away from the face she was sculpting and saw herself in the cracked window three and a half feet up the door. This was her sanctuary, where the person she really was came out for a few hours. She tried to compress her time to compensate for lost days and months when she'd been another person, for somebody else, trying to bring happiness and obligation together, like giant cables one in each hand, forcing their exposed wires into contact. It was not easy and she should have been aware in advance.

A photo album of her wedding was still around some-where but that was about all which remained. That dress, the nights out before the big day with best friends, and bridesmaids enjoying 1970 through her. Top tables, seating plans and vegetables she'd never liked, stood out from the hazy setting of the day itself. She remembered running along the strand at Donabate the day before with Milly Vaughan and Carmel Brennan. 'This is it,' they thought together as childhood started up going going gone and they were all gung ho and Babychammed up to the nines. It was the day of days, the sun peeped through but now that could have been a heat wave where they shimmered in the glimmer and felt ten pounds slimmer. Mrs. Cody was going to perm her hair first thing Saturday and then they'd be off, driven into the unknown in a Ford Capri. A champagne car for the price of lemonade! Like an ambulance races into the future that red car, with a wing mirror gone, was their airplane to happiness. "Sure of it Milly, sure of it." We are the girls with our hands on the rails of the Waltzers at the fairground. Something had hovered over her in the minutes while she'd waited for the lift from her cousin Paul. "If only your daddy could be here to see you Catherine." Her mother held her at arm's length and said nothing about what might lie in store. Carmel Brennan had a baby in the Rotunda Hospital two days after Bloody Sunday and she told Catherine the secret of womanhood. "Never ever tell your daughters about the pain of childbirth. That's the secret Cathy, that's why women go on and on and men become cowards. The most important thing about us is that we can become mothers and still we never tell each other what it's like for the ones who haven't yet experienced it. It's like a painful recipe for wonderful soup; we can't forewarn others and yet we all want to make that broth." There was more though, stuff she'd never dreamed of until she began to have nightmares about it; the violence, the psychological warfare, the bloody-shameless let-downess of it all.

"I thought I'd explained all of this to you before?"

"I know, I know I just forgot that's all."

Out away beyond her now she saw the back door open and her mother stood in the space and called down at her to come up for her tea. She could have been seven years old again and fielding the invitation from the swing made of knotted rope and inch-thick board. Tilting her head she squinted and made her mother smaller as though projecting her in time to where *she* was small and Catherine held the comfort keys; tea; story; change; bed.

She had started a piece about a year ago which had begun as an idea to sculpt her father (fifteen years after his death on a building site in the city centre) as he might have looked now had he lived. He had a brother called Jimmy who was two years younger than him and she hoped to use some of him for the aging process to gauge the changes her dad might have undergone. Photographs of him playing football for Home Farm in the fifties would augment her research and she'd planned to make him look a little younger than his age would actually have been. Artistic license took many forms and she felt sure that love and affection and loyalty were ingredients in the composition of that license. In the end she became so upset when she'd tried to begin to carve that she'd stopped after an hour or two. She realized that the research end of things was some-how arm's length and not too difficult, but the creative process, when it began, exposed the rawness of loss even years later and made it impossible for her to continue. That had surprised her.

"THE PILL; ON OR OFF PRESCRIPTION?"

"Several East European Doctors felt that it was important to keep the Pill on Prescription because that meant that doctors would have access to women in the reproductive age groups in order to carry out routine health checks like breast examinations and cervical smear tests."

"Can I ask you something Catherine?"

"Yes Carmel."

"Is everything okay between you and Chris?"

"Sure. It's fine, everything's fine. Why? Is there something that seems wrong?"

"No. No. Well I suppose I just wondered about the mark on your cheek."

She touched it. "This? Oh just a silly accident. I was bending down to put something in the fridge and I must have taken my eye off the door because it swung…"

"SPECIAL OFFER ON DOORS AT McCORMACK'S FURNITURE AND HARDWARE ON THE LONG MILE ROAD."

She loved the smell of mothballs. It brought her away from the present in an instant. It transported her back over the bumps and hazards of twenty-five years or so. It comforted her on the journey and got her there in one piece to her grandfather's pharmacy in the west of Ireland in a small village in County Galway. There she would always be a child, breathing in the scent of bottled remedies and bath crystals which hung in the shop like clean clothes drying near a fire. The blue jars, with names she couldn't read, sat in rows like armies of glass on the shelves waiting to be called into action. She'd sat on a high stool in the back of the premises on endless Saturday mornings while her mother's father filled prescriptions and measured powders into paper funnels and then handed them to the emissaries of the people who were sick. An open fire burned in the shop and people were drawn to it in search of solutions.

Her eyes would sometimes water at certain smells but the overwhelming scent which she carried away from that time was of mothballs. It was a smell you could taste as it carried you up and out over the mundane world beyond the jangle of the shop door. She recalled the baize-lined trays with dozens of single lenses with their small handle grips. These were the tools her grandfather used to bring sight to the aged and the squinting. He would work for hours with his clients, patiently listening to their opinions about whether lines on the illuminated box on the wall were now darker or lighter with each change of glass. Out of their uncertainties he would forge an understanding and, consequently, a mix of thickness and contour which would open up the world to them once more.

"Maureen Potter at the Gaiety Theatre."

The marriage had been a disaster from the beginning. Once he'd hit her across the face on the balcony of the hotel in Gran Canaria she knew it was not going to get any better.

He'd had all sorts of problems himself and yet nothing was ever his fault. She'd overheard a man in a pub once tell a joke about domestic violence;

"What do all forty thousand battered wives in Ireland have in common?"

"I don't know"

"They just wouldn't listen." The laughter still rang as clear as if those men were right beside her now. Chris was a soldier ; all eyes front and physical-fitness grading and an endless stream of courses in the Curragh Camp which taught him how to assemble small arms in the dark. She'd never understood what it was he actually did for a living. Like a runner practicing for a race that never happens, the closest he got to what he was trained for was a month of border duty every now and then. Searching cars for arms and illegal fireworks at Halloween wasn't her idea of job satisfaction but it seemed to touch the mettle in him and he loved it. At least he loved something she thought. They'd met in a dancehall when he was stationed in Dundalk and she had been given a commission by the Electricity Supply Board to sculpt a bog-oak exhibit for their new offices there. Her mother had travelled up with her to the opening of the building and then retired to the bed and breakfast while Catherine and her cousin Nonie (who'd come for the spin) spent some of the money on dinner and a night out.

The rain on the roof began again and she turned the plasticine face on its swivel base and pondered about what might be within this head if it came alive. Could it really provide her with whatever it was she needed? And what was that? Friendship, companionship, challenging debate, a resurrection of the dreams she'd put away in a box in the attic with a dusty off-white dress she'd sold herself in? Who knows what lies behind the noses and doors of others? Not her. She'd enough of his promises now that everything would be different if she stayed with him and how he hated himself for hurting her. It was rare enough that he acknowledged his own guilt but even when he did it was always qualified, never clear. He apportioned blame in every direction; she'd driven him to hit her but if they worked at it together they could avoid a repetition.

"KILKENNY SEMINAR STRESSES LOVE IN LASTING MARRIAGES."

Back in her reserves of good or neutral times she'd saved chunks of her childhood in jars with the mothballs to consume again when there were lapses in her life. She'd never had brothers or sisters the way most people she knew did. It was always just the three of them; Mam, Dad and her. Even her cousin, Nonie, who was her closest friend since they were kids, had drifted away with Milly and Carmel after Catherine married Chris. Her dad's accident was like a fence stake driven into the dirt of her life and her wedding day was the next point along the wire. Between them lay a time which was not always happy but *was* always safe. Back beyond her father's death lay a deliriously contented portion of her life which had promised happiness indefinitely but had been overtaken by events. When it *had* just been the three of them she'd fitted in, like a tiny flower between two larger plants. They had been a family which had not looked outside itself for fulfilment. She remembered the creak of the pantry door each Friday as her father returned home from work and swept her in up his arms so she could scrabble her way through his pockets for the sweets or treats that pay-day prompted.

She watched the last of the rain evaporate from the path and opened the door of the shed and stepped out into the late afternoon. The door clicked shut behind her and she began to walk up the path weaving her way over the cracked tarmac to the milestones on that journey; the bordered flower bed and the cat's bowl.

"WEAVER'S HALL IN DERBY SHOCK."

A flash memory came to her as she took the two steps up to the back door in one stride. She was very young and there was someone standing, no sitting, adjusting a webbed belt or was it leather with pouches. She was unsure as to whether this was a genuine memory in its own right or a composite of reality and film or dream and picture-book. Her mother was standing near the hatch from the kitchen into the sitting room. The kettle had boiled on the bread-board it called home and the steamy drops of water falling from the underside of the row of cupboards overhead had almost ceased.

"Mam?"

"Yes Love?"

"I don't know if I dreamt this or made it up or if it's true or not or just mad but…"

"Yes?" her mother turned to face her with a packet of Marietta biscuits in her hand.

"Did we ever have a Russian soldier living upstairs in the spare room when I was a child?"

Her mother's face blushed for an instant and then she replied, "No, no Love, we never had a Russian Soldier living upstairs in the spare room. What made you ask that?"

Catherine began to wash her hands in the sink.

"I don't know. Maybe it's just being tired with all that's going on at the moment but I had this picture in my head of a man sitting on the bed in the spare room and I came up the stairs and saw him and he looked up and smiled and he was in a uniform and he was doing up his belt."

Her mother lifted the kettle and began to pour the boiling water into the teapot. In mid-pour and with the water gushing she spoke again,

"We did have a *German* Soldier; well a pilot actually, living in the spare room for a while. Maybe that's what you were thinking of Love."

Orchids

~

It was the perfect summer's day. Bees hopped in and out of roses and the dog-daisies craned their necks in the breeze like nosy neighbours. In the sky the sun restrained itself so that the heat was bearable and the clouds hustled past on the horizon on their way to shop for raindrops. The serious whisper of leaves in the full of their health shushed the afternoon like a worried chorus and their voices came and went in the way sleepy children might hear the world through an opened window.

Somewhere else, but near enough to see and hear and enjoy the afternoon, the high walls of St Muiredeach's Home for the Criminally Insane rose like a hologram out of the countryside. You could have searched for hours and never found it or just as easily have stumbled across it in a momentary wrong turn on a Sunday drive. It was that kind of place. Once the country retreat of a rich Dublin family, it was now the jewel in the crown of the Mid_____ Health Board. This splendid house, made from the pain of peasants in the 1820's, lay surrounded on three sides by a lake. The only road in or out was over a narrow bridge of cast-iron by which one crossed the small stream which bisected the strip of land which linked it to the rest of the country. It was mid-July now and the rhododendrons and hydrangeas out-did themselves all around the garden of St Muiredeach's. The blasts of colours and blooms gave the whole place a splash of normality and a casual visitor might have been forgiven for mistaking this institution for an hotel.

In an office in the heart of the main building Dr Raymond Horrigan, psychiatrist, clipped his long nails with a small scissors and looked out a window onto the lawns. He could see one of his patients, Crowley, sitting on a bench by the small pond which was full of goldfish. There was a strong wire mesh over the top of the pond and Crowley rolled up small pieces of bread from a bun into tiny balls and flicked them onto the metal net. The flurry of water in the aftermath of each throw showed where the fish gathered to compete for the food. Behind the bench two male nurses stood chatting. Each nurse was at least six foot five and Dr Horrigan knew that they would need all of their strength and power to restrain Crowley if he were not kept on his strict regime of medication. He smiled to himself as he remembered the words of his predecessor, Dr Costello, when he'd retired and given up this swish office,

"Raymond, our job is not to cure. Our job is to baby-sit. And, as we all know, babysitting is easiest when the babies are asleep."

The office was big by comparison with the others in the building. It housed a large handmade American Oak desk and, along one wall, a table large enough to seat eight at a pinch. On the other side of the room was the mandatory couch for patients and a large reddish leather armchair with huge button studding which had sides at the top of the back, boxing in the luxury of occupying it. As he clipped, the small bits of nail fell onto the carpet under the window ledge. The ledge was large enough to sit on and if he knelt on it, and looked as far right as possible, he could see the small car-park at the end of the complex and know at a glance who had arrived late or gone home early. The lawn was bleached in parts by the undeserved sunshine they'd enjoyed so far that month.

On the far side of the garden the perimeter wall was pockmarked here and there by small weeds which grew where there appeared to be no holes in the binding concrete. Sunlight hopped off the pond surface and the reflection of the mesh on the water created the effect of a crossword puzzle trying to fit into place. Crowley got up timidly as one of the nurses leaned over his shoulder and tapped their watch in front of him. Raymond Horrigan glanced behind him into the body of the room and his eyes settled on his framed primary degree parchment from University College Dublin. He made no attempt to clean up the nail clippings and simply put the scissors back into the top left-hand drawer of the desk where they kept company with pencils he never used, an inscribed pen from his last posting and a spare set of keys. The drawer slid back into its burrow just as the telephone on the desk beeped and a red light appeared over the word "reception." He pressed the speaker-phone button.

"Yes Carol?"

"It's Mrs Fay Doctor. She's just arrived."

"Great. Send her up."

"Will I ask Mr Reynolds to send one or two?"

"One should be enough Carol. I've read the file. Have Mr Reynolds send Mike or Robert and tell them to remove the cuffs before they bring her in okay?"

"Yes doctor."

He looked at the black and white photograph on the front of the file. She looked about thirty-five, averagely pretty with a touch of overdoing the make-up. He re-opened the folder and skimmed down through his notes. The word "*Orchids*" was written in large letters in his own hand. He recalled from his reading that on a questionnaire she'd been asked to fill in, during the psychiatric assessment for the trial, she'd written "Orchid" as the answer to every single question. There was a knock on the door. He sat down and covered the file with some other papers. After about three or four seconds he answered, "Come in."

As the door opened he had an emerging view of her. She was taller than he'd expected and much more striking than the photograph had implied. The nurse who accompanied her stood directly behind her and Horrigan presumed it had been he who had opened the door.

"Mrs Fay Doctor," said the nurse. Raymond Horrigan rose slowly from his chair and beckoned her into his office,

"Do come in Mrs Fay. I hope you had a pleasant journey from Dublin?".

She did not answer but stepped in over the door saddle and walked into the centre of the room. He held out his hand and, just as he assumed she was going to ignore the gesture, she took it and shook it gently. He could see the nurse outside the door with the expression which questioned whether he should come in or remain outside.

"Mike will be outside the door if you need anything Mrs Fay." The nurse closed the door.

"It's wonderful weather we're having," said the psychiatrist. "We've been waiting since last year really."

He felt that he detected a slight smile playing on her lips. He wondered if she would be one of the hard nuts to crack; the silent morose types who looked on him as an inferior or as someone doing his best but to no avail. Or would she be overtly hostile and eventually play right into the hands of the control he exercised over her? They were all different in their own way (or course) but there was a subplot to all of them which mended the torn emotional cloth they each came to St Muiredeach's in and rendered them uniform in their expressions. They were like abandoned kittens or stray horses. Sure they all had stories and backgrounds and histories and case details which varied, but it all amounted to the same; some sort of discount-bargain life which had ended in the misery of others. He paused and then offered her the couch,

"Perhaps you would feel better lying down." As soon as he'd formed the words, and let them off at her, he imagined a sexual undertone and instantly sensed just that misinterpretation of the phrase by her. The trace of a smile he'd suspected earlier re-appeared and she stood still and looked him up and down as though he'd just asked her to dance. There was a further silence now and he was beginning to feel uneasy when he remembered the questionnaire.

"I understand you have a fondness for orchids?"

Her face transformed into a genuine smile and her body seemed to ease into a less threatened (or less threatening) stance. She rubbed one of her eyes with the back of her hand and then spoke for the first time.

"Odontiodas are best in this climate. They are cool-growing and suit greenhouses where the temperature is usually lower."

The ice was cracked if not broken and the UCD graduate made the next move.

"We have lovely gardens here and we always welcome any expertise our…" he searched for the word although he knew it rather well, "our *residents* may have to offer."

He saw her looking past him to the window and although it had no bars he knew its reinforced glass would present a problem for her if she tried to jump through it. Years of experience however made him quite sure that she was no risk. Of all criminally insane candidates, those who murder a spouse or partner are generally no danger to society at large and most probably not even to themselves. Raymond Horrigan knew insanity when he saw it and he doubted if he saw it now. Her file indicated a history of violent abuse by her husband which had culminated in her murder of him as he slept. Clever lawyers had realised that the provocation defence was not going to be much help and had instead opted for the loony line. Temporary insanity would not work and so a trawl by a sympathetic shrink through her school diaries and a couple of letters she'd written herself did the trick. If she were truly violent she'd be in Dundrum. Saint Muiredeach's was the open prison (without the openness of course) to which lesser members of the criminally insane fraternity were sent.

"Would you like to look at the gardens?" he invited her towards the window.

"Aren't you afraid I'll jump to my death through the glass or try and escape?" she smiled.

"I'm prepared to take that chance," he replied with a half laugh.

She was gorgeous he thought as they stood side by side and looked out the window of his office. He lingered a gaze on the outline of her breasts through her jumper and felt the beginnings of interest below his own waist. Her face framed the side of the window sash and he was aware of her taking in as much of the garden as the window allowed, like a thief in an art gallery memorising the position of cameras.

"Orchids enjoy the light Doctor but not the sun's direct rays. I think that the corner behind the pond would be the best place for them. Could we build? I mean would they let me, would *you* let me have a lean-to or a small green-house?"

He sensed that this was a time to be generous and so he moved to put her at her ease,

"I've already made enquiries about a Perspex greenhouse and you'll probably need blinds as well?"

"To control the shading, yes. On bright days you know the blinds will be down from nine am to five or six in the evening. Vandas and Phalaenopsis can be harmed by sudden bursts of strong sunlight." She had used the future tense in relation to her stay in St Muirdeach's and Horrigan knew he'd won.

"I'm afraid I don't know much about orchids," he said easing out some more leeway to her now so that she could relax as the person among them with the edge in some interesting but safe topic.

"Perhaps you'll let me teach you a little?" she smiled and they turned together and walked towards the door. He longed to touch her but knew he could not.

The nurse took her gently down the corridor and waited until Horrigan shut the door before putting on the handcuffs for the journey to her room. Horrigan liked that because it gave him an opportunity to forge a link with the patient at the expense of the staff. They were on the same side now and he sensed that in time she would open herself to him like a flower. By the time he discovered the spare keys and the scissors from the drawer were missing it was too late; Mrs Fay had disappeared without a trace. They said the male nurse who had tried to stop her taking the postman's bicycle would never see out of his left eye again.

Clocks and Snow

~

"Miss James?"

This quiet enquiry, from near the foot of the ladder upon which she stood, beckoned the librarian's assistant back from the dust of the 1865 All England Law Reports into the midday moment of the second Tuesday in December in the Squire Law Library.

"Yes Mr Blunden?" she replied, stepping down two rungs in one movement. She caught a paper clip which the retreating volume of Law Reports dislodged from the shelf edge in front of a neighbouring tome as it slid home sideways. She quickly and effortlessly saw that all was well on the shelves below as her journey neared its finish.

"I'm off out to lunch Miss James. I shall be back at say…" he hesitated as if really leaving the hour of his return to chance. "Five minutes to one," she mouthed silently, in absolute synchronicity with his gentle announcement, before turning round to face him as her flat-soled shoes touched the floor and she straightened her plain grey skirt in the same movement.

"Very good Mr Blunden, I'll see you then."

"Yes," he agreed awkwardly.

He took three steps backwards on a tiled floor he knew by heart and then changed direction, straightening up to face the main double doors just as he reached the carpet border which framed the deep rectangle of the central reading area. She watched him and knew that exactly twenty two steps from the front desk would take him to the outside world, and that included the one and a half steps to the side when he pulled the left door open and paused in case anyone should come around the corner from the cloakroom. Whenever someone did, he always waited and held the door even if he'd only heard their footfall and they were seconds away across the other side of the tiled hall beyond the mosaic of the faculty crest and motto in the centre of the floor.

Wilfred Blunden had been Head Librarian in the Squire for nine years now. He'd been working in the library in one capacity or another for nearly thirty years having begun in the late 1960's as a teenage runner ferrying books on his bicycle all around the University in response to neatly written requests from students and lecturers alike. He walked to work from a small house on Barton Road where he lived with his mother. He wore the same cuff-links every day (of silver Highland Terriers) and he always placed his trilby on the top of the filing cabinet when he came in, which was odd because beside the same cabinet was a hat-rack no-one used. He drank tea at eleven and four from a red flask he kept in the bottom drawer of his desk and he always went home for lunch at five past twelve and returned on the dot at five to one. Although they'd worked together for almost four years this was pretty much all Elizabeth James knew about him. He was her boss she supposed, at least in that formal sense of superior rank and experience, but he treated her as an equal in every respect and never told her what to do. She liked that about him.

Her previous job in the City and Guilds office in London had been a nightmare of bureaucracy and egos battling for superiority in a shabby building near Victoria Station. She was glad to be miles from there now and had in fact been surprised to get the job when she'd applied after seeing it advertised in a Sunday newspaper. Her tasks at the City and Guilds had included maintaining the library and that shard of experience, plus a good interview, had seen her into the new position ahead of at least two other candidates she knew of. They had been interviewed before her and she remembered that awkward five or ten minutes, before the interviewers arrived, when she and the other two had just sat smiling politely at each other from chairs ringed around a small waiting room in the faculty building in the Old Schools. She recalled vividly the other two; a fresh good looking blonde boy with strangely mismatched eyes (one blue, one green or was it one brown, one blue) and a tall matronly lady in her sixties who wore glasses which kept

slipping down her snub nose. They'd nodded and acknowledged each other over a coffee table crammed with the Law
Gazette and Cosmopolitan, each of the candidates occasionally glancing over at the door into the office where the real
battle would take place. She'd been delighted to get the job
as it allowed her to move away from London at the time
when she most needed to. A six-year relationship (with a
three-month engagement period tagged on at the end) had
finished only a few weeks earlier when the Chartered
Accountant of her dreams had decided to balance the books
of some smart HR executive he'd met on a "team building
weekend". A couple of drinks at a conference centre in
Berkshire had set the scene. They'd married shortly afterwards in the Bahamas and now lived in Chelsea. Perfect.
She remembered his obsession with Formula One motor-
racing and regretted all the Sunday afternoons she'd wasted
waiting for the cars to go fifty or sixty laps on television
while Murray Walker chatted merrily into a microphone
which came out of the side of his head. She'd wasted a lot
more than a couple of Sundays on Nick Cameron. An awful
lot more.

Cambridge was gorgeous. She often thought of this
town as a replacement lover in her life, wrapping itself
around her in the winter and walking along the river with
her when the sun came out. She was thirty-eight now and
all her school friends were either married or out of touch
with her in some other way. Visits home, to the stone walls
of that place in Yorkshire where she'd left her childhood,
were no longer enjoyable. She'd grown tired a long time

ago of being everybody's aunt. In a period of about 18 months, a few years earlier, she'd been a Godmother three times. These people had asked her then to stand for their children for all the right reasons however everyone else declined to ask her now for all the wrong ones. These days she came to work and did her job and loved it, but at the weekends she made arrangements with older women she hardly knew to go to church fetes she barely enjoyed. Mrs Williams, who ran the Charity Shop around the corner from Elizabeth's house in Mill Lane, often called in to see how she was and drank endless cups of tea until she agreed to go with her to some village hall the next weekend and run the cake stall. She meant well but she was thirty years older and lived for that kind of thing anyway.

Mr Blunden was practically the only man she spoke to now and their relationship was entirely on a professional footing. He was handsome enough in his own way but he lived a life which did not seem to have either an entry point for outsiders or much room within even if they'd managed to gain access. She'd never met his mother but she could see that he was devoted to her. She phoned him at work occasionally when there was a domestic crisis, like the time she dropped her house keys down the drain outside M & S. Double-fronted doors of the Squire marked the meeting point of the separate worlds of Elizabeth James and Wilfred Blunden.

Today was different. Elizabeth had decided to buy the Cambridge Evening News and to read the "personal ads". If a newspaper had contained the key to her job why should it

not provide her with the opportunity to complete the trans-
formation of her life? She'd often glanced at the "personals"
before but until that Tuesday she hadn't really begun to
realise that out there somewhere might be the person for
her, someone who too perhaps was isolated in their own
world and trying to reach out beyond it and themselves. She
couldn't place an ad herself, no, that would be too forward,
but she *could* read the entreaties of others who needed someone and see whether what she wanted, and what they
offered, matched. She did not want to be alone for another
Christmas. The very thought of buying the paper that afternoon, and reading it with purpose, filled her with a twinge
of excitement she hadn't felt for a very long time indeed.
Mr Blunden returned from lunch and she went to the Blue
Boar for soup and a sandwich. On the way back she bought
the newspaper from a seller outside the post office in Trinity
Street. The narrow street was crowded with shoppers who
gazed into the Christmas displays in shop windows. A tired
set of lights ran in a flash along the inside of the window sill
in a book shop and the blockbuster titles stared out into the
afternoon like puppies in a pet shop pleading for a home.
Elizabeth James didn't dare to open the newspaper but
simply placed it carefully in her handbag, between a retired
compact and an address book she'd had since school, and
looked forward to reading it after work. A timid smile
played over her face for an instant as she mounted the steps
back to the library from the Senate House Square where a
young couple were stealing a kiss behind an elegant pillar.
When she returned Mr Blunden was standing beside a pile

of Admiralty textbooks which was almost as tall as himself. She read his distress immediately and went to assist him in stacking them on the reserved shelf even before unbuttoning her coat for the afternoon ahead. She glanced at the huge clock on the balcony.

"Thank you Miss James."

"Not at all Mr Blunden, I'm sorry if I'm a little late back from lunch," she apologised as the last volume was housed by his expert hands.

"That's quite all right Miss James. You're not late at all. I must get the porter to look at the clock. I'm sure it's a little fast."

"Well-built farm worker seeks milk-maid for harvest." was the "Ad of the Week" and it was written in bolder type than the rest as a reward. By and large the "personals" were either suggestive or badly written, or both, and were almost certainly not penned by the type of person whose company she might hope to keep. Miss James steeled herself with some fresh tea and began the column which followed on the next page. She read through the advertisements one by one with her red pen at the ready. By the end of the section she still hadn't made any marks. In a moment of disappointment she scanned the next page with its "Classic Cars" and "Books and Magazines" sections. Her attention was drawn to a small captioned pair of two ads under the category of "Social and Professional". This is more like it she thought.

Her neatly hand-written introductory letter to "Single Professional gent seeks refined lady 30–45 years N/S with

GSOH," went by the morning post on Wednesday. When her eye glimpsed the back page of a newspaper, which said Cambridge had beaten Oxford in the Varsity rugby match, she felt it was an omen. Mr Blunden seemed strangely distracted that Wednesday and more than once she noticed him staring absently into space. This was most unlike him. Normally Mr Blunden's work was his life for the entirety of the day, however he was clearly preoccupied.

"Are you all right Mr Blunden?" she enquired politely as he poured the afternoon tea from his flask for himself.

"Yes, yes I'm perfectly all right Miss James, why do you ask?"

"You look a little pale that's all. Shall I open a window?"

"I think I might have a touch of flu," he ended the conversation. "There's quite a bit of it about."

He wandered off in the direction of the index-card filing drawers and she wondered if she'd left one of the windows open earlier in the week and given him a chill. She took the long window-pole with the hook and began to inspect the alcoves.

Two days later Mr Blunden's mother died. On Monday one of the cleaning ladies, whose sister worked in a doctor's surgery on Mill Road, brought the news to the library. Mr Blunden hadn't come in that morning.

"It's the funeral to-day. Cremation's at eleven twenty."

"Oh," said Elizabeth. "I hadn't realised. I don't know what to do really."

"Probably best to do nothing, death's a funny business," Iris leaned against the handle of the mop to force all the water into the cold grey steel bucket with its frothy lip. Elizabeth felt strangely helpless and wondered how she should greet Mr Blunden when next she saw him. She supposed he probably wouldn't come in for the rest of the week or so. He arrived in that afternoon just after four.

"I heard about your mother. I'm so sorry. I would have sent flowers but I didn't know until this morning. Is there anything I can...?"

"Thank you Miss James, your condolences are very kind indeed. I'm afraid there's nothing to be done really," he sighed. "Has that new Environmental Journal arrived?" He placed his hat on the filing cabinet and began to unbutton his coat.

"Yes, yes it has. They delivered two copies and I sent one to Mr Feldman at the Faculty Office."

"Thank you Miss James," he said sitting down at his desk. He lifted his gaze for a second to meet her kind expression and she saw that he had been crying. Behind him, outside through the oval window which overlooked Gonville and Caius, it was almost dark.

A reply arrived on the 18th of December. The handwritten envelope was the only post she'd received for over a month and she instinctively knew what it was even before she'd deciphered the smudged local postmark.

"Dear Miss James,

I was delighted to get your letter. I have been away on business and although I have had a number of replies yours is the only one to touch my heart at this, the most precious

*time of year. I suggest a meeting in the Hat and Feathers pub
on Barton Road at 6 pm on next Friday after work. I shall
be wearing a blue suit with a University tie-pin and match-
ing lapel badge. If this suits, no need to reply.*

    Yours, Robert."

She was thrilled. After years of loneliness she felt that she
was at the edge, as it were, of a new beginning. She knew
from his handwriting and from his tone that he was a kin-
dred spirit. Christmas *was* a precious time of year, how right
he was about that. Would he be handsome? Dashing? Tall?
Successful? It really didn't matter because she knew that it
was what was on the inside of a person that mattered and
between the lines of this wonderful reply lay the shadow of
a good person with a kind heart. They could not fail to find
common ground. She was sure of it.

All around the town now Christmas drew in and the
cackle of terrified geese in the back of a lorry reminded
her immediately of it all on her way back from lunch on
the appointed day. Elizabeth never wore a watch so, in her
eagerness to be punctual for her "date", she brought the
small black travel clock from her bedside table to work in
her pocket and set it by the clock on the balcony.

Mr Blunden had overcome his bereavement or, if he had
not, he gave no outward signs of his grief beyond that one
unguarded moment on the afternoon of the funeral. It was
impossible to know what he was feeling inside and Elizabeth
had other things on her mind. Shoppers bustled past each
other to get into shops where rosy faced assistants feigned

enthusiasm and sprayed perfume onto wrists. The Christmas tree in the Market square oversaw the continental quilts in their plastic wrappers as strange hands turned them over and tossed them back at each other. The students were about to go home and the University golf announcements in the window of Ryders and Amies went out of date without anyone noticing.

She had cycled to work that Friday and her red bike, with it's tired tyres and creaking wicker basket, waited for her chained to some railings outside the library. She hurried home at five and showered and changed. She'd been up at seven to wash and dry her hair and now, with her overcoat collar turned to the wind, she pedalled past the Chemistry Department. It was bitterly cold and she stuffed her gloves into one of her coat pockets and then blew on her hands before pushing open the door into the pub. The chatter of the crowded bar spilled out to her and she could not hear individual voices at first but her senses adjusted as she walked into the heart of the room. She spotted him at precisely the same time as she saw from the clock over the cash till that it was only ten to six. He was tall *and* handsome but her heart fell when she watched as he glanced furtively around the room before removing a plain gold ring from the wedding finger on his left hand. He slipped it into the breast pocket of his jacket and then rubbed his finger as if trying to remove a stain.

Elizabeth walked over and stood beside him while she asked the barman for directions to Granchester. The mark on the man's finger was shiny, a different colour to the rest of his hand. He gave an oily look past her towards the door and she smelled the faint aroma of aftershave. She never wanted to smell it again. He had no idea that she was the person he'd come to meet and that was simply because the clock on the balcony was ten minutes fast. She moved away from him now, in a daze, to the door back out into the world she'd expected to be leaving behind.

On Christmas Eve at around noon it began to snow. The small puffy flakes swirled down around the roofs and arches of the University town and settled brazenly on the ground. Elizabeth had busied herself for the previous week by inventing work that barely needed doing. She worked longer hours than she needed to and tried to think of something happy but could not. At two-thirty they locked up together and prepared to leave the library. She saw him now as if for the first time, this lonely gentle man who'd lost his mother two weeks before Christmas. It was a moment in which she glimpsed something more of herself too.

"Mr Blunden?" she began as he clipped the window-pole back against the wall.

"Yes Miss James?" He turned to see her taking her coat down from the hook by the stairs. She shook it purposefully.

"I wonder if you would care to join me tomorrow for Christmas dinner?"

The Last Straw

∽

Mary typed his pleadings and his letters and now, after thirty-eight years of service, she was giving up to nurse her husband who had suffered a stroke five months earlier. He'd been buying shoes in a small shop on Henry Street when other customers noticed him trying to put a black brogue on over his own shoe. The shop assistant who came to help had barely managed two or three words of the 'what-seems-to-be-the-problem-sir?' variety before Mary's husband had collapsed on the carpet talking incoherently and crying. He imagined how she would cope with nursing him and trying to bring her life's partner back from the place just out of reach which he now inhabited. He would miss her calm efficiency and the weekly note on top of his typing which offered to make any amendments or corrections over the weekend on her own time. There were never any corrections necessary. She'd found him a replacement of course, as he'd known she would; a share in someone else's secretary. All computer discs and e-mail. In truth he'd not had enough work to keep Mary busy full-time for years but she'd masked that decline for him by paying herself less and less as the years wore on and pretending to need more time off than she really did.

It was just the nose-end of August and the sun was a friend he treasured more now than when he'd been a child. The 'long vacation,' as it was called, meant two months of waitressing in America or para-legal work for the very young, a chance to catch breath and tackle paperwork for the people in the middle, but it was never quite clear what it meant for the old hands like himself. When he had had lots of money, in his forties and fifties, he took grand holidays in Tuscany and the Lake District, pampering himself and his family with villas which were too big and clothes which always seemed too small. They made friends with people who rented next door and invited them to Dublin for New Year's or for landmark anniversaries which were a couple of months hence. These people never came to visit and he knew that it was because the invitations had always fallen short of being completely genuine. Not spite or falsity or a desire to mislead but rather a compacting of those people into that foreign time and leaving them behind really. Among the huge grey stones with white swirls which his children collected on beaches, and the recipe you insist you must have but never get, these short-term intimate acquaintanceships were abandoned on the last day in the rush home to the kennelled-out dog and the uncut lawn.

Victory in small cases in obscure courts had given way to the middle ground of well paid defeats where insurance men smiled couldn't-care grins into yawns. He recalled a golden period, twenty odd years ago now, when he had more work and cash than he could have dreamed of. It was a haze of meetings, cases, cheap highs and expensive lows when people winked congratulations or winced in sympathy after trials which had run and run and had sometimes got away altogether. He had been, if not king, then at least crown prince. His was the name junior barristers wanted beneath their own on the Plenary Summons. He guaranteed profile, high fees and the promise of more. Nuggets about his way of running cases filtered through the coffee of a generation of people behind him. His closing speech to the jury in a huge libel action was the template for a dozen less eloquent finales and a handful of better results. People said he worked without notes and for a while he did because he wanted to, now he sometimes went without notes because he had left them at home or on the train. Most of his class-mates from the Inns were gone. Some had retired years earlier having made it onto the bench. Others had died and he felt that, frankly, some had simply been mislaid. They were to be found at christenings occupying armchairs and reminiscing about an imagined past which no-one cared to contradict. Some had invented better degrees or different universities for themselves. Others talked non-stop about "The Law" as if it were an old friend who had respected *them* in return. The five or six who were still at the Bar now with him were nearly all Senior Counsel. He'd made the jump before most of them and had outlasted all but this handful. Some of his time was spent remembering the people from his class who had been older and had been hoovered out of the library by Time and Death. He had no recollection at all of some of his time in practice as it seemed to have greyed and been swallowed up by landmarks like illnesses and weddings. Some of his own children were now in their forties and he had one granddaughter who was already a year or two in practice on the Eastern Circuit. He was old and beginning to sense it.

One afternoon, years before when he was approaching forty five, he'd had an opportunity to be unfaithful to his wife. A woman who had been at college with him approached him and asked him to act in her separation proceedings for her. He'd sorted her out with a solicitor who didn't charge and he himself provided his own services for free as well. They managed a very decent settlement of the case which was favourable to their client. Months later on that strange afternoon in November she'd paged him at the Law Library and he'd taken her to have some tea. Over the chipped cups in the downstairs restaurant she casually mentioned that she was staying at the Westbury Hotel for a couple of days while her house was being rewired. She placed a hand on his own on the table and asked if he would be interested in spending the night with her. He'd fancied her at university and might once even have been in awe of her but not now. Not like that. He'd been more surprised than shocked but had composed himself and laughed it off. Now thirty years later his wife was dead and no one asked him to spend the night with them in hotels. He supposed that it was all a question of timing.

Rain had been forecast on the radio bulletin the night before but all around Dublin the sun bounced its heat at the streets and the people. A cheque had arrived in the post from a firm of solicitors he'd never heard of. Scrutiny of the headed paper revealed that they'd devoured a smaller firm ('Incorporated' was the word they used to describe that repast) and this was money owed from a case he'd been in almost five years earlier. Cheques were the medals in the sport of the hunt for Justice. He looked at the amount and decided it was a dead heat for bronze with about a dozen others. When some people wanted you to get the papers drafted they could live in your pocket, annoying you into action, but as soon as the case was over they were impossible to contact and very slow in paying. His most valued obstructing solicitor, a gruff man from the West with a big heart, had retired some time ago now and although they occasionally met for a game of golf he knew that they'd really drifted apart when the solicitor's son had taken over the practice and ceased to brief him. It was all enormous conveyances and glitzy chancery opinions from barristers who had office-suites and skied more often than they appeared in court. No more decent trip-and-falls and battles of wits with parsimonious insurance-panel colleagues. The watch words now were hourly billing and photographs in the Solicitors' Gazette at bogus conferences in South Africa.

When he'd been called to the Bar in 1954 it was considered touting to get the papers back to a solicitor within six months!

The garden was peaceful because the children from the house behind were gone away to summer camp or somewhere. Their excited screams made gardening impossible because he always felt that flowers should only be tended in silence. He still liked it though when a football sailed over the wall and onto the lawn. Kicking it back from his hands touched memories and nerve-endings about schoolboy matches and the mayhem of under-eight rugby practice, so so long ago now. For him the summer meant shaky umbrellas and a hastening reduction in his own levels of vigilance against saying the wrong thing. He had a clear picture in his mind of a huge beach where his brother had been treated to a donkey ride while he had sat out a sentence on the low step of the promenade for some misdemeanour. Stairs creaking in his grandparents' house, linen covers for the arms of the armchairs and the scent of fuchsia which he loved still. He'd found a coin while sitting out the treat and it gave him the whiff of fairness.

In the early days he'd been flat broke. He'd worked in pubs in London and building sites up and down the motorways to save some money for the following year. Gradually it eased, though he could not pinpoint the moment he'd become solvent. He didn't care much for money but he did feel the pinch when it was scarce. He'd lived in flats before they were given notions and called apartments. He'd taken his wife to the Laytown races in 1961 and won enough money to give them a week in a hotel in Listowel at the end of the summer. He could still smell the rashers which drifted on the air up the back stairs to the huge room they'd been able to afford. They'd spent all the winnings and had been winners a dozen times over during the week in Kerry away from the children.

A brief had arrived on the previous day and he'd resisted opening it to exercise the semblance of not having to address any paperwork during the vacation unless he wanted to. Now, as the sun dipped behind evergreen trees in a churchyard some way off, he opened the long slim envelope and read the covering letter. He laid the envelope on the rain-eaten table surrounded by potted plants and stone figures which had been there when they bought the house.

Somewhere back in the past he'd had strange dreams, roundabout the time his eldest daughter had been doing her final Med exams. He had fallen into a pattern of sleep which frequently found him waking while still trying to achieve something in the dream. People flew past him and he measured them in strands of light against each other or ached as people he wanted to talk to disappeared from view at that critical waking moment. He had been worried, his wife told him, but they never managed to figure out what it was. Cases merged with each other and the big case against the maternity hospital became confused with the legal-aid brief in the Special defending Ireland's heroes against a State they refused to recognise. There was a joke somewhere in the back of his mind where the punch-line was the judge telling the Accused that he was entirely correct in not recognising the Court because they were in temporary occupation of the school hall while the courthouse was being renovated. He couldn't remember if he'd found it funny the first time he'd heard it.

Birds twittered in the hedges and he looked up but could not see them. The remnants of a cup of tea quivered as his knee knocked against the leg of the table. He spread the papers out and pinned down the edge of three of them with the side-plate. They were leases of some sort relating to land in County Wexford. Their client had a dispute over the rent payable as he was allowed a credit against his payment resulting from the delivery of straw to the farmer who owned the fields. The amounts of money involved in the dispute were tiny. Why would the solicitor send the case to a Senior Counsel? He resolved the question with the feeling that there must be some complex issue of title to be determined despite the apparent simplicity of the case. Adverse possession, Overstint, Encroachment, all of these doctrines came back now, each moving aside to make way for the next as they were considered and then dismissed. His wig was in the Law Library in his locker. The smart tails of the Senior robes hung almost touching the steel floor. Below the robes old envelopes and photocopied precedents were jammed against each other; reminders of old and great and awful cases. The ghosts of colleagues who had negotiated settlements with him, or taken him short, or done him turns, lurked in the robing room in Dublin 7. The uniform was waiting for the first Monday in October to begin its work again.

Dusk intruded now and a glow over the carnations in a window-box on the lawn allowed the old barrister a moment to look directly at the sun as it disappeared. The papers lifted at the edges and began to slap on the wooden table as they became more adventurous. A door inside the house slammed as the breeze gained unlawful entry though the French windows. He could hear someone calling over the fence, but it was difficult to discern whether or not those words were meant for him. On the apple tree they'd planted almost a half-century ago, when the twins had been born, the leaves rustled and encouraged fruit to fall. The people in the hospital had done everything they could. There was no doubt about that. How could you live and work with the responsibility of life and death every day? He bet no-one on a ship or an aeroplane had ever heard the announcement "Is there a lawyer on board?" and he chuckled at his own joke. His mother had lived to see him take silk. The rain had belted down on them for the photographs. He was unsure whether 3 or 5 judges had sat in the Supreme Court that day but he knew it didn't really matter. Now he felt the breeze on his face and his eyes began to close. Somewhere far away his wife was calling him in from the garden.

Mr Hop and the Last Post

～

It was the day before Christmas Eve in Highgrass Meadow. In the kitchen at number five, deep beneath the old oak tree, Mrs Hop was baking her famous carrot pudding. Upstairs in his bedroom Mr Hop was using his favourite carrot-shaped pen to finish his letter to Santa Claus. He had begun to write his request weeks earlier but had kept changing his mind so often that he had almost left it too late to finally get his letter done.

"Hop?" his mum shouted up the stairs.

"Yes?" Mr Hop answered.

"You'd better hurry and finish your list if you want to make the last post," Mrs Hop stirred her pudding mix once more for good luck.

"Okay Mum I'm nearly done now," Hop licked the envelope. "Do we have any stamps?"

Mrs Hop shook her head and looked at the sieve. Hop was so forgetful that he wouldn't remember his own name sometimes if it weren't written on the labels inside his clothes.

"Under the statue of the Bobtail Ballerina on the mantelpiece Hop, where they always are," she sighed.

Hop bounded down the stairs and grabbed his woolly hat from the hook where it hung near the last step. It was cold out and he knew that his ears would get chilly if he didn't cover them up. He pulled a long red scarf out of the drawer of the telephone table in the hall and wrapped it around his neck. One end got caught in his left foot and the other jammed in the drawer as he shut it so that, in the end, he tripped himself up and landed with his tail in his mother's favourite potted plant.

"Hop! What *are* you doing to my plant?" Mrs Hop snapped as she came out from the kitchen drying the carrot flour from her paws on her apron.

"Nothing Mum," Hop said, getting up and fixing the scarf. He turned for the door and was about to open it when his mum's voice stopped him. "Stamp!" she said. Hop stamped his foot.

"No, no," said his mum. "A stamp for your letter."

"Oh I forgot." Hop turned around again into the hall and narrowly avoided another disaster with the potted plant. Hop's mum lifted the statue of the Bobtail Ballerina and licked the last remaining stamp in the Hop household before sticking it on the envelope Hop held in his paws. She read the address:

"Santa Claus.
The North Pole
Quickly"
and smiled to herself.

"Is that the last stamp Mum?" Hop asked.

"I'm afraid it is Hop but we don't write to people very often so we shouldn't need more stamps until next year."

"But what about *your* letter?" Hop asked.

"*My* letter?" His mum seemed puzzled as she fixed Hop's scarf.

"Yes Mum, your letter to Santa."

Hop's mum stopped fiddling with his scarf and became very serious for a moment. "I'm afraid I don't send letters to Santa anymore," she said sadly.

"But why not?" asked Hop. "How else will he know what you want for Christmas?" Hop could not understand why his mum seemed so sad.

"A long time ago Hop, before you arrived, before The Crows moved in upstairs, before we even had a proper suite of dandelion armchairs, I did write a letter to Santa and posted it on the day before Christmas Eve."

"And what happened? What happened Mum?" Hop asked. His mother's eyes filled with tears and her tiny earrings of eight-carrot diamonds jingled lightly. "Nothing," she said simply.

"Nothing?" said Hop.

"That's right," said his mum. "I never heard a word from Santa and the thing I asked for, which I didn't think was too much, never arrived on Christmas morning."

121

"Did you ask for something different the year after that?" asked Hop.

"No," said his mum. " Because I hadn't got a reply from Santa I figured that if he was too busy to read my letters, then maybe I would become too busy to write them. So I never wrote to him again."

"But he always answers my letters by bringing what I want at Christmas," said Hop.

"I think that's because you're young Hop. You're only a small rabbit and maybe Santa is just too busy to bring presents for adults." Hop saw that there were tears in his mum's eyes.

"Don't worry Mum," he said. "I'll open up *my* letter and add in a few things for you before I send it." He was about to rip the envelope when his mother laid a paw on his and stopped him.

"It's too late for that now Hop. I haven't written to Santa in twenty years and I doubt if he'd even remember me. You'd better hurry or you'll be too late to post your own letter." Mrs Hop opened the door of number five Highgrass Meadow and sent her son out into the chilly December air on his way to the post office.

At the top of the meadow a path ran along beside a stream which ran in the opposite direction. Hop hopped along the path until he came to the thick ivy bushes which contained a small opening that led down a slope to the village of Twisty Wood. The whole place was lit up with Christmas lights, from Mr Hoot's General Store to the offices of Mr Weasel the auctioneer. At the top of the street a flashing sign outside

Miss Hedgehog's acupuncture clinic announced *"One shopping day left"* and the shelves of nut and berry muffins in Aunt Squirrel's shop window begged to be eaten.

"Hello Hop," said Maggie Otter rushing by with her shopping bags full of presents.

"How's your mum?" asked Herbert Hare with a wink from behind his vegetable stall as he tossed Hop a carrot.

Hop wanted to stop and chat to everyone and to soak up the thrill and smell of Christmas but he could see from the clock on the church tower that it was nearly five o'clock so he hurried on his way. Mr Stoat the Postmaster was about to pull down the blind on the counter window when Hop entered.

"Hello Hop," he said. "You're cutting it a bit fine aren't you? Another hare's breath and I'd have been closed."

"Sorry, sorry," said Hop a little bit puffed. "Am I still in time to post my letter to Santa?"

"Of course you are," laughed Mr Stoat. "In fact the post-van driver, Mr Mouse, has just phoned to say he's running a little late this evening. They had a flat tyre down at Ponding and they've only just fixed it so we've plenty of time. Why don't you come into the sorting room and put it in the sack yourself?"

"Can I really?" asked Hop. He was ever so excited.

"Of course," said Mr Stoat. "I'm going to light a pipe for myself and I'd better do it by the back door in case Mrs Stoat comes down. She doesn't know I still smoke."

Mr Stoat shut the main door of the post office and then he and Hop went into the sorting room together. Hop had never seen anything like it. "Wow!" he said as they stood in the middle of the floor with huge sacks of letters and parcels piled all around them waiting to be collected and delivered on.

"Here's the one you want," smiled Mr Stoat pointing with his pipe at a bright red bag with the name 'Santa Claus' written on it in white letters with bells and holly drawn inside each letter. Hop stood on his hind legs so that he could stretch right up till his nose was almost inside the top of the bag. He popped his letter in. They turned to leave the room.

"What's in there?" Hop asked, noticing an old door in the corner which had a pile of out-of-date telephone directories and the Orange Pages stacked against it.

"That's the old sorting room," said Mr Stoat. "It hasn't been used for years since we built this extension when they closed the post office in Fogarty's Falls".

"Is it locked?" Hop asked, eager to explore. Mr Stoat smiled to himself and remembered that when he was a young stoat he had loved to explore exciting new places.

"I'm sure there's a key around here somewhere."

"Oh great-floppy-ears," said Hop excitedly.

'Creak.' The old door groaned and moaned as it opened for the first time in ages. Cobwebs were stretched and spiders ran for shelter as they were disturbed by Mr Stoat's firm grip on the door handle. There was no light-bulb so Mr Stoat shone his big winter torch in so Hop could have a look around. There were old heavy stamping ink-presses and large folded cloth mail-sacks which had long since been nibbled through.

"It's pretty dusty in here," said Mr Hop sneezing his way into the centre of the room. "Achoo, achoo, achoo." His woolly hat was covered in cobwebs and the end of his scarf scuffed up a trail of dust as it dragged behind him.

"It's not been opened in years, this room," said Mr Stoat as he puffed his pipe in the doorway and continued to shine the torch in front of Hop so that he could see his way. Out from behind Mr Stoat came the sound of the post-van arriving at the back entrance to the post office.

"You'd better come out now," said Mr Stoat. "I need to lock this room and help load the sacks onto the lorry." Hop began to slowly make his way out of the old sorting room when suddenly his eye was caught by a bright object in the beam of the torch.

"What's that?" he asked.

"What's what?" asked Mr Stoat.

"There, just at the edge of the light."

Near the corner of the room, under the weight of an old stamping press and between it and the skirting board, Hop spotted a white square. Mr Stoat shone the torch and Hop bent down and dislodged it. It was a dusty envelope with one corner of it shining bright where the tassels on Hop's scarf had disturbed the dust. Hop handed it to Mr Stoat and, as they closed the door of the old sorting room together, Mr Stoat blew the rest of the dust from the letter so that he could read the address.

"Well I never," he said.

"What is it?" Hop asked.

"It's a letter to Santa and, if I read the date properly, it's almost twenty years old. Here have a look." Mr Stoat handed the envelope to Hop and Hop could hardly believe his eyes. From the shopping lists he was given each week he recognised the handwriting straightway.

"Oh great purple turnips!" he exclaimed. "This is my mum's handwriting."

"Well I'll be a hazelnut," said the Postmaster. "She must have brought it here to post it but somehow it got lost behind the old stamping machine. She must have wondered what happened to it." Mr Stoat took back the letter and had another look at it.

"She missed the last post," said Hop. "That's what happened."

"And she'll miss the last post again if we don't hurry," said Mr Stoat. Behind them out in the yard the van was revving its engine and beginning to drive away.

"Quick," said Hop. "Give it to me."

He snatched the letter out of Mr Stoat's hand and hopped as quickly as he could down the steps into the post office yard. He bounded across the cobblestones after the van and, as the driver hesitated before turning right and out onto the main road, Hop managed to grab on to the tow-bar with one paw. With the other he held his mum's letter over his head and threw it at the red post-bag marked "Santa Claus" and saw it sail in. Bull's-eye. Mr Stoat clapped as Hop made his way back to the post office.

"Well done young Hop, you made the last post by a whisker."

On Christmas morning Hop awoke to the sound of his mother crying with joy and cheering and hopping around the house in delight.

"Hop, Hop," she called. "Come downstairs and see what Santa's brought!"

Hop was downstairs in a jiffy and his mum stood in the middle of the living room swirling about in her dressing gown like the Bobtail Ballerina herself.

"What is it Mum? What is it?" Hop asked. His mum took him by the paws and danced him around the room.

"He got my letter, Santa got my letter, he really really did."

Hop looked at his mum to see if she was wearing some new earrings, or a necklace but she wasn't. He peeked in the kitchen to see if she'd got a new toasted carrot-maker or a china scraper or a parsnip tweaker, but no. What could she have asked Santa for?

"But Mum," he said. "I can't see…."

"Look," said Mrs Hop taking his paw and leading him to the front door.

She threw open the door. Now Hop saw what it was that his mother had asked for in her letter to Santa years earlier, before Hop himself had arrived, before The Crows moved in upstairs, before they even had a proper suite of dandelion armchairs; it was snowing. Bright white flakes were falling from the sky and the whole of Highgrass Meadow was a blanket of fluffy, wonderful, beautiful snow. Hop looked at his mum and saw that she wore the most excited expression he'd ever seen on her face.

"Happy Christmas Mum," he said.

"Oh Hop," his mother replied. "I think it's going to be the happiest Christmas anywhere."

Kerosene Verling

~

The town was not yet in view by the time the sun began to set. Out across half of Utah State the open expanse of dry earth was a repository for wild things, a place where loneliness was the only welcome and where water almost never occurred in a quantity of any use to man. It was a little cooler now and the only sound was the "clop clop" of the horse under Kerosene Verling. He was a small man. Some people talked him up to about ten feet tall but those who did so had never met him. Anyone who did come across him was usually struck by two inescapable physical features; his small stature and the gap where his right earlobe had once been. There were a dozen different stories about how he had lost part of his ear but again these were rumours and myths dipped in exaggeration. The truth was that the only other person, apart from Kerosene, who knew what had actually happened, was dead.

He slowed his horse and began to sense the night closing in on them both. He had a fair idea of how far they'd travelled and he expected the lights of Christian Falls at every moment. He wondered to himself whether he would be aware of the very last step they took before the place was visible. Could he then make his horse take a step back and have the town disappear from view or would it be visible for a long time before he could see it? Take four different men or women and stand them in a straight line walking and he guessed that no two of them would see it at precisely the same moment. He thought of gunfighters and of how no pair of them were ever exactly the same speed. How could they be? There was so much between the first step out onto the street and the last man standing; you had to hesitate, anticipate and then draw and cock your pistol and aim and squeeze the trigger and hope and pray and sweat and then close your eyes and wait for the verdict. He remembered the words he'd heard spoken by Sledge Dalton when he, Kerosene, had been only thirteen or fourteen and still called Jude;

'Don't try to get off more than one shot. If you do, you'll think you've got two chances when the truth is you only ever have one.'

Kerosene could see the town now; a little sparkle at horizon level where goodness prospered and multiplied. He could smell the cooking, he could even guess the colour of the icing on the cakes in the front window of Alvarez's Bakery. He hadn't been there in nearly fifteen years but he found it hard to believe that anything much might have changed. There was a picket fence about two feet high around the church where Reverend Kain preached each week about sin and repentance. It was as though the fence could keep in captivity all of the wrongs the townspeople carried with them to Service and then, like some cleansing turnstile, allow the people themselves out again to resume their lives with clean slates and light hearts. It seemed implausible to him that if God really did exist that He would have chosen to make his home in Utah. Why not Chicago or Philadelphia, where the climate was more varied and the clothes more sophisticated? He'd even heard that most men in those cities did not feel the need any longer to wear holsters. God would be much safer in Philadelphia, Kerosene reckoned.

About five years earlier, when he'd been in prison in Mexico, he'd met a man who'd passed through Christian Falls on his way to Arizona. He was a mean-faced man who always seemed to be on the verge of falling asleep standing up the way horses and cows do. He said his name was Reuben but it probably wasn't and anyhow it didn't matter. What was of interest to Verling was that he'd seen Verling's home town more recently than Verling had.

'Stayed in a boarding-house across from the General Store.'

'Mauds?'

'Don't rightly remember the name but there was this pretty young thing running the show, she had some set of....'

'What was her name?' Verling cut across his path to coarseness.

'I don't know, Raphez or Rosie or summin.'

'Rachel?'

'Could be it was, I ain't so sure about her name but, tell the truth, names don't interest me much.'

The man had enough of a memory to satisfy Verling's curiosity. It had been his only ration of information about his sister until three weeks before now when a letter had tracked him down to a bar in San Jose. He'd given the name of the place to Mr. Bakis, the schoolteacher in Christian Falls, in case anyone ever needed to find him. After a decade and a half of silence Verling assumed that if his old teacher deemed it necessary to write then it must be pretty damn important. Verling could write a little but he couldn't read much and so the ex-confederate- Major who ran the bar read the letter to him when the place closed at about four in the morning.

"Your sister has been the victim of unwanted attentions by two or three local men and she is with child. The Sheriff seems unable or unwilling to take any steps. I fear for the safety of your sister and her unborn baby."

"Unwanted attentions," was the phrase which stuck in his heart. It was the closest Mr. Bakis would ever get to saying what had really happened; the truly brutal acts which had prompted this crisis. Verling had seen enough of that kind of barbaric violence against women in the course of his own life. He knew the path which led whisky-sodden gut-less cowards to perpetrate harm. He'd been guilty of many things himself in his time, but not that. His own life was no menu of saintly acts; he'd been in trouble and prison and had ridden to Hell and back a couple of times. He'd also killed eleven men in the time he'd spent alive so far. He'd heard that number cranked up to fifty by drunks in saloons who didn't know what they were talking about or who they were talking to. What did it matter really? Once you'd ended someone's life for the first time it became a little easier. He'd heard folk say that gunfighters placed little value on life and that was how they could kill and kill again. Kerosene Verling reckoned different; what higher value could you place on one life, your own, than a willingness to kill others to allow that life continue? It was a living.

He was so near the town now he could touch it but that was as close as he wished to be that night. He swung right, off the main track, and headed for the copse of trees above the schoolhouse. He tied up Horace using a careless twist of the rein on a branch which they both knew the horse could easily escape but would not want to. This routine marked the closest thing he'd ever had to friendship with anyone or anything. He made a small fire to the leeward side of an old corn barn and drank coffee until he was too tired to drink coffee any more. He unrolled his bed from the saddle pack and slept with his pistol in his hand inside his shirt where the metal stole some of the warm progress the coffee had made. A cricket shouted about his return to anyone who was listening, but almost nobody heard.

'I let myself in.'

The voice gave the old man a fright as he distributed grammar books to the empty desks before the noise of nine o'clock had had a chance to steam in from the yard. He jerked his head and saw Kerosene sitting in the corner on a chair reserved for pupils who misbehaved.

'Jude,' the teacher turned his hands palms upwards as though carrying an offering. 'You got my letter?'

'I did, it was very civil of you to let me know what's happened.'

Kerosene rose from his seat and advanced to greet his old tutor. He felt the man's gaze on his ear and on his gun-belt before they shook hands in a meeting which made both of them uneasy.

'How is she?' Kerosene caught the teacher's glance with a look of his own as they disengaged, each unsure of what to do with the hand that had shaken.

'I wouldn't have written Jude unless I was afraid for her. But you'll forgive me, I hope, if I tell you that I've wished that letter unsent a thousand times since I put it in the mail.' He looked down at Kerosene's pistol again and then glanced to the window through which children could now be seen climbing the railed steps from the road below.

'You did the right thing Mr Bakis but I need the names of those men. I really need to know who did this.'

There was no threat between these men now, just a gulf of expectation and a few little shards of regret. The older man was in the eye of the storm and knew that what he had always expected, from the instant he'd taken pen in hand, would happen now one way or another. It had seemed so clear then, and it still did, the right and the wrong of the thing. What he had not prepared himself for was the sight and sensation of the situation righting itself. He'd spent thirty years telling children the difference between right and wrong and explaining that nothing wrong could ever be right, nor the other way round either. He picked a piece of chalk from the ledge under the blackboard and wrote three names in white. The gunfighter was more concerned about disappointing his teacher then exposing his own inability to read and he made a show of screwing his eyes up as though he needed spectacles.

'Daniel Maine, Sam Carlsen and Hunter Carlsen,' intoned a chirpy eight-year-old girl who was first in to class that morning. 'Like the new real-estate company.' Both men turned to see her and a sad smile passed between them which saved the honour of the teacher and his former pupil.

The Carlsen Lumber Yard was on the western edge of the town. It was a great sprawling enterprise which had eaten up all of its competitors with an ease and enjoyment which had made most decent folks wince in pain and despair. Little by little, with the assistance of the Western People's Banking Corporation and its Manager Daniel Maine, the lumberyard had choked the life out of the surrounding businesses. Kerosene strolled past the window of the real-estate offices of the men he was looking for but he did not know it. He left his horse outside the weary-looking Silver Saloon and began to walk in the middle of the street towards the prosperous arch under which anyone for eighty miles who wanted lumber had to pass.

He remembered the brothers from his childhood; sociable enough when separated but fuelled by danger and hatred when they worked together. He had enough pictures of them in his head dredged up from years ago to recognise them straight off when he saw them poring over a scale model in the office. He announced himself past the desk of the typist who put up one hand like she was taking an oath and clapped the other to her mouth to stop it escaping.

'I believe you're in the real estate business now?' Kerosene said calmly.

'Yes, yes we are. Can we help you in that regard?' the younger one said as the other lumber king pulled a Derringer from his sleeve. Absolute fear had now jumped into the room and covered the two blonde boys.

'Two burial plots please!' Kerosene Verling drew and a single shot took the face off the man wielding the little gun. He paused to allow the other man witness his brother's death then he re-holstered and watched the newly-bereaved eye up the shotgun leaning in the corner behind the desk. Verling stared him out for twenty seconds and then turned to leave. He anticipated the gaucheness of the timber man and swung round and dropped to one knee as the shotgun butt jammed against the wall when the remaining Carlsen sibling wrenched at it. Verling cut him in two across the waist with three shots fired quickly enough to be over before the shotgun coughed redundantly up at the ceiling and made a pretty pattern in the corniced plaster.

The Bank was full of people who had seen the flames from the lumberyard. He expected to see the Sheriff and some deputies waiting for him but, in retrospect, he reckoned they probably preferred to engage in some safe and fruitless posse-work later on than to risk immortality in Main Street. Verling asked to see the Manager and arranged for the redemption of his sister's mortgage on the boarding-house. He then watched the Bank Manager place a revolver barrel in his mouth and pull the trigger. There was a dull 'snap' as life absconded and Mr. Maine's last thoughts met the framed Finance-House licence on the wall behind him. Kerosene had not been at all surprised that the man agreed to end his own life in exchange for those of his wife and children; after all business was business and Maine had a talent for recognising bargains.

That winter Kerosene Verling met a man who was faster with a pistol than he was. Two days later, on Christmas Eve, his sister gave birth to a boy she named Jude after someone who had vanished from her life forever years earlier, when the summers were hot and the grass grew as tall as a gunfighter.

November Eves

~

November Evenings ! Damp and still
They used to cloak Leckhampton hill,
And lie down close on the grey plain,
And dim the dripping window-pane,
And send queer winds like Harlequins
That seized our elms for violins
And struck a note so sharp and low
Even a child could feel the woe.

Now fire chased shadow round the room;
Tables and chairs grew vast in gloom:
We crept about like mice, while Nurse
Sat mending, solemn as a hearse,
And even our unlearned eyes
Half closed with choking memories.

Is it the mist or the dead leaves,
Or the dead men–November eves?

James Elroy Flecker (1884–1915)